Pathogen:
Patient Zero

Kai Kiriyama

xoxo
Kai
Kiriya

To John

"What's your Zombie plan?"

[signature]
xoxo

ISBN: 1507851790

ISBN-13: 978-1507851791

Kiriyama

To those forgotten,
And to those left behind.

Kiriyama

DENIAL

"Oh God, someone help me!"

I had fallen asleep in the car as my dad drove me to the hospital. I'd fought him for days, saying I was sick, I had the flu, there was nothing to worry about, but he won in the end. My parents always won in the end. I had been sleeping way more than was strictly necessary and I'd been running a fever off and on for days as my body tried to fight off the infection I'd picked up from God-knows-where. He finally forced me to get up and walk down the stairs. I'd been asleep for three days. I hadn't eaten anything for five days, and I was having trouble keeping basic fluids in me.

My mom was panicking at home, apparently I hadn't even been drinking anything as I slept. I didn't remember anything of the sort. I didn't remember mom trying to force me to drink at least some Ginger Ale. I don't even remember getting up to go to the bathroom. I remember sleeping and feeling feverish and awful, and that was it. According to my dad, Mom had started freaking out when she came to check on me and she thought that I had died in my sleep. She said I looked like a skeleton, that I'd lost too much weight and that the dark circles under my eyes had scared her into thinking I was dead.

So Dad loaded me up into the car, in my pajamas and slippers, no less, and had decided that it was for my best interest that I go to the hospital. We were chatting, Dad was filling me in on why I was being dragged to the hospital in my mismatched pjs, without a shower or any sort of warning, and telling me what I'd missed happening in the house and the news since I'd been sick. He joked that the Toronto Maple Leafs had won the Stanley Cup and that I'd slept through my birthday. I told him to shove it, and that I was feeling really feverish and kind of carsick and I just wanted to sleep more. I leaned my head against the window and passed out again as we drove.

It didn't take long to get to the hospital, I knew that much from all the times we'd had to drive there in the past. It was about fifteen minutes away from my house, which was a good thing because I was accident prone, and Dad parked at the emergency entrance. He was already panicking before we'd gotten there. My fever had spiked again and my skin had flushed. He tried shaking me awake, but I was too far gone. I could feel him shaking me, and hear him shouting at me to wake up, but all I could manage was a weak groan and an "uh-uh" before fully passing out again. I was dead to the world, and even my dad trying to get me out of the car didn't wake me.

"Hey! I need help!"

If I hadn't been buckled, I'd have fallen out of my seat when my dad opened the car door. Thank God for road safety. I groaned again and the world started to spin. I could barely open my eyes, I was so tired, I just wanted to go back to bed. The spinning refused to stop and I felt hands grabbing at me, pulling me out of the car. I felt my feet touch a solid surface, which I assumed was the sidewalk. I couldn't open my eyes, everything hurt and the spinning refused to stop. People were mumbling around me, nonsense words that I couldn't understand.

I opened my mouth, trying to speak, but my words slurring into a drunken garble. I really didn't feel good. There was a metallic noise and I was moving forward while the world was spinning.

"Hey?" I managed to grumble. "I'm gonna..."

I didn't get to finish my sentence before I was doubled over, retching and emptying what little I had left in my stomach all over the sidewalk. I only managed to stay upright because two sets of strong hands held on to my arms and shoulders. Someone patted my back as I heaved.

"Oh, God..." I mumbled, opening my eyes just a little as the nausea, and the spinning, subsided.

On my right, was my dad. On my left, however, was the cutest orderly I had ever had the pleasure of laying eyes on. I felt a heat rise up in my chest and threatening to colour my face as I realized that I had just hurled up bile all over the sidewalk, and probably on the orderly's shoes.

"I'm really sorry," I mumbled, trying to hide my face from the cute guy on my left. He was like a god made flesh, and he should have been in the movies, instead of helping me into a wheelchair. Man, was I ever embarrassed.

"Hey, don't worry about it," he replied, patting my shoulder. "Happens all the time, and at least you missed my pants."

His gentle and jovial nature did nothing to make me feel better. I was sick, smelled like I was dying, and just puked on the sidewalk in front of the cutest guy I'd seen since high school ended. I mean, yeah, I'm only eighteen, but that never stopped me from appreciating anyone's looks before. I just wish that we could have met on a day where I wasn't making a habit of throwing up in public. I could have used a boyfriend.

I sat in sullen silence, trying not to pass out again as they pushed me through the hallways and into a private room. It was unusual, I didn't think that our insurance was as good as it seemed to be, and I didn't want to make a stink about where they were taking me, just in case this was a mistake and I'd be forced to go into the waiting room with every other sick person in emergency.

"Your doctor will be with you shortly," the cute orderly said, flashing me a smile.

Dad said something that I didn't hear, I was too busy being completely mortified by the fact that I'd just been sick in public.

"You really didn't need to bring me to the hospital," I muttered.

"You're sick," Dad said. "You need to get better and I'm going to do whatever I can to make you better. If that means dragging you to the hospital so you can puke on that cute nurse's shoes, then dammit, I'm gonna take you to the hospital." He held me at arm's length, forcing me to look at him.

I was confused. I wanted to laugh, and cry, and crawl into a hole to let the flu burn me up and then die. I did the first two, instead, barking a rough laugh that turned into a choking sob of embarrassment and gratitude.

"Oh, sweetie, don't cry," Dad said, wrapping an arm around me in a sideways hug. "I could tell you stories…"

"No thanks," I assured him. "I don't need my stomach to turn again."

"Your loss, I have some really good drinking stories from when I was younger. And none of them involve a hospital."

"I'm gonna die."

"Of embarrassment?" Dad asked.

"More like of starvation," I replied with a smirk, though the tears running down my cheeks said I wasn't quite as cocky as I was behaving.

"Pfft," he spluttered. "You'll get some saline and some crackers and some antibiotics and you'll be right as rain. Then we'll go have a pizza the size of New York, and you'll get fat and then blame me for ruining your girly teenage figure.

I stared at my dad for a long moment, sniffling and wiping the snot that was threatening to drip from my nose on the back of my hand. His eyes showed me how worried he really was, even though his words said that he wasn't. I forced a smile and wiped the rest of my tears away.

My dad was probably the strongest person I knew, and if he was sure that I was gonna be okay, even with his paranoia, then I had to hope that he was right.

"Thanks, Dad," I said with a small nod. I sighed and wiped at the drying tears on my face. I must have looked awful. Not only had I started out looking gaunt and skeletal, now I was all red and puffy from crying.

I hoped that the cute orderly didn't come back to check on me, I don't think that I could take any more embarrassment in one day.

As my dad sat there holding me in one arm with me leaning against his shoulder and dabbing at the tears against my cheeks, we were suddenly joined by a handsome doctor.

"Hi," he said awkwardly. "I'm not interrupting am I?"

I blushed harder than I did when I puked on the orderly's shoes. This doctor had to be in his thirties, easily, but he had the charming demeanour and classic good looks of someone who played a doctor on a crappy television sitcom. I was instantly smitten and embarrassed as hell.

Why was it my crappy karma to be surrounded by the cutest doctors in the world when I was sick and embarrassing myself left, right and center?

"No, not at all," I choked, suddenly very self-aware. I was dressed in the ugly paisley hospital gown and my thin cotton pajama pants with cupcakes on them. Really colour coordinated and fashionable. Not.

The cute doctor smiled at me. "I'm Doctor Alexander," he said. "You can call me Liam if you like."

Liam Alexander. I started considering myself with his last name.

Wait. Was I fantasizing about marrying the doctor in charge of my case? My God, was I like 12 again or something?

"Hi," I mumbled.

"So I hear you're not doing too good?" he asked me.

"It's just a flu," I replied. "I mean, I was looking at colleges and stuff before I got sick, I probably picked it up from one of those dirty hippie kids on campus or something."

"Hey, I was one of those dirty hippie kids on campus," Doctor Alexander said with a grin. "Well, I mean, I wasn't exactly dirty, but I sure wasn't the most normal kid there."

I eyed him suspiciously. "That's hard to believe."

"Oh, it's not once you get to know me," he replied. "I was all into the new age, hippie, homeopathic medicine craze. Still am, but you know, there's better money to be made using actual science and medicine. At least until society catches up with the idea that there's other forces at work in nature, and that science has barely begun to scratch the surface of what the primitive people knew about medicine."

"I still don't buy it," I teased. "But I mean, historically seeking, yeah, the old cultures knew a hell of a lot more about the way the world worked than we give them credit for. Who knows what they knew about medicine? Most of European history is fraught with superstitious bullshit that was only heightened by the introduction of Christianity while the rest of the world was making miraculous advances in science and medicine..." I stopped talking and shut my mouth hard enough to make my teeth clack together.

Doctor Alexander was far too easy to talk to.

Doctor Alexander laughed. "Wow, for someone who has been as sick as you have, you're really bright. History major, right? With a minor in mythology and religious studies? Gonna go into teaching or something when you're done?"

I shrugged. "Maybe?"

"I think you'd be brilliant at it."

"Thanks..." I muttered, so embarrassed. "So, what do you think I have?" I asked, changing the subject back to our business. "I was already cleared for the basics, tuberculosis, and AIDS and cholera and all that," I said. "I've been sick for a while, like three weeks at this point, with varying degrees of severity in my symptoms, and we went and got a bunch of blood work done already when nothing seemed to be breaking this. I'm pretty sure that it's just a flu."

Doctor Alexander smiled again. "Well, it's hard to say for certain," he said slowly. "We're gonna give you another round of antibiotics and do everything we can to clean you up and figure out what's making you sick."

I nodded. "All right," I agreed reluctantly. "I'm feeling way better today though. I slept for three days solid and I feel like I could run a marathon."

I had to stifle a cough as I said it. Stupid bad timing.

Doctor Alexander grinned. "Fair enough," he said lightly. He stepped closer to me and took out a penlight. He shone it in my eyes, down my throat, in my nose and ears. It was awkward, but not the worst thing in the world. At least I wasn't naked.

13

"Well, I think you have a major fluid and mucus build up right off the top," he said. "If that's all it is, it's probably a sinus and lung infection. A round of antibiotics will clear it right up," he explained. "Doesn't explain the vomiting, though, unless you're just having a bad reaction to the pressure, then I could that having just been a side effect of motion sickness. I'll send a nurse in to get that started right away. It'll be an IV drip of antibiotics and saline, try and get you hydrated again. If that's it, you should be out of here in a few days."

Dad nodded and patted my shoulder. "See, kiddo? Nothing to worry about."

I smiled bravely, trying not to embarrass myself any more than I already had. I was crushing hard on Doctor Liam Alexander. I'd never call him Liam if I could help it. Not out loud, anyway. That would give me away as a fan. Doctor Alexander nodded and smiled and left us alone.

"That wasn't so bad!" Dad exclaimed happily. "Told you it wasn't anything serious!"

"Dad," I said flatly. "I was the one who was convinced that it wasn't anything serious, remember?"

Dad laughed, it was a sound of sheer relief and nervousness. "Yeah, I suppose you're right," he agreed easily. "But still, it's awesome isn't it? Your initial diagnosis and it's a good one? You're one tough cookie, and one lucky kid, if I dare say so myself!"

I nodded. "Yeah, I know," I agreed.

I sighed. This was insane. But hopefully, a round of intravenous drugs and some extra vitamins and saline would flush my system and fight off this infection and set me up to be right as rain in a few days. "Hey Dad?" I asked.

"Yeah?" Dad replied. He'd been lost in his own head for a few moments and I had to wonder exactly what he was thinking about.

"Thanks for everything," I said. "Thanks for bringing me here to get the medical attention I need..." I shrugged and felt more tears welling up in my bloodshot, puffy red eyes. "I really appreciate it and it means the world to me that you trust me like that."

Dad smiled. "You're welcome," he said. "But don't worry anymore about that stuff, okay?" he instructed me. "You just focus on getting better. Antibiotics work faster if the recipient is willing to let them work, you know."

I laughed, "You just made that up!" I accused.

"Maybe, but it sounds good, doesn't it?" Dad said.

Laughing and shaking my head was a bad idea, it caused myself a round of pain, followed by the need to cough up a gob of gross green phlegm. "Eew," I mumbled as I got up to get a tissue. I went to the washroom and washed my hands and returned to the bed next to my dad.

"I really don't want to stay here overnight," I admitted.

"I know," he replied. "But they want to keep you for observation, make sure you're getting all your fluids and stuff."

I sighed. "This sucks."

"You want me to stay?"

I shook my head. "No. You need to go and do damage control."

"Do you want a book or something?"

"No. I want to sleep."

Dad stood up and kissed my forehead. "I'm gonna head home then, okay?" he asked. "Mom and I will visit you tomorrow."

"Yeah, sounds good," I said with a sigh. "Get outta here before I change my mind."

He kissed me again and left as the nurse entered with an IV line.

"All right," I said, holding out my right hand to the nurse. "Let's do this," I said, sounding far braver than I felt.

The nurse didn't say anything as she worked. She snapped the rubber band against my arm, tying it too tight for my comfort, and then jabbing the needle unceremoniously into my tender flesh.

"Ow," I complained. "Be careful, I'm not a practice dummy."

The nurse rolled her eyes. I made a mental note to complain about it.

"Your veins are probably collapsed from dehydration," she said with no trace of remorse or apology. "It'll be uncomfortable until they reopen and you're properly hydrated again."

"Uh-huh," I replied bluntly.

She pulled the needle out of my arm where she'd missed my vein and tried again. I watched her with mute fascination and horror as she missed another three times before she finally found my vein. She placed a square of the rough, clear tape they used in hospitals against my skin to hold the IV line in place. I watched as my skin puffed and swelled and turned purple with bruises underneath the tape. I was just glad she finally got it; otherwise I'd have taken it away and done it myself. Not that I knew how to, exactly, but it couldn't have been as hard as she was making it out to be,

This girl was all good looks and no charm, though. I wondered how she had gotten to be a nurse in the first place. Her bedside manner was undesirable, she was obviously not interested in talking to me, and she was too made up to be serious about nursing.

I sighed and tried to not give her a piece of my mind about how much nicer she should be and how much more careful she ought to be when putting the intravenous lines into other people's hands.

"Is there anything else I can do for you?" she asked flatly, as though she was bored and unimpressed with me.

"If there's a book kicking around somewhere, I'd love to read something," I asked, trying not to be sarcastic. "But otherwise, maybe just some water and a ginger ale?"

She smiled at me, a cold smile that suggested that I was lower than a piece of gum on her shoe. I would definitely request that she not come back. I hoped that she wouldn't, either.

I smiled politely, flashing my teeth. "Thank you," I said as she turned on her heel and left me alone.

I settled back against my pillow, and pulled the thin sheet and blanket up to my chin and closed my eyes. I hoped that the drugs would kick in and kill whatever was causing the infection in my everything, and that I'd be home again within a few days. That would be nice, I decided. And then, maybe after, I could go for coffee with Liam, as a thank you for healing me. Mom would love that, wouldn't she? I grinned and felt a brief giddy rush of elation thinking about the possibility of taking an older, handsome doctor out for a coffee date.

I felt myself nodding as I slowly drifted off to sleep thinking about Doctor Liam.

ANGER

My parents came to visit me in the hospital the very next day.

I sat weakly on the bed, feeling tired and stupid for being admitted to the hospital because of a flu and a lung infection. The room was boring. I was in a private room, at least. Lucky me, I guess. The walls were a dark brown wood paneling on the lower half of the wall and a gross hospital mauve on the top. At least there was no tacky wallpaper. And even better, there was no cheery art reproductions. The room was bland and bare. I had a window overlooking the parking lot for my natural light quotient and a thick door separated us from the rest of the hospital. There was an observation window that looked out into the hallway, but my mom had insisted that we keep the blinds drawn so that no looky-loos could gape in at us.

I had been woken up at six in the morning to get some blood work done, and have a quick look over from the doctor.

I didn't embarrass myself too badly this time. I did tell Liam that the redheaded nurse who gave me the IV the night before should never set foot in my room again. He agreed to that and promised I'd have a better nurse next time.

1

I also made sure to keep that little tidbit of information from my parents.

They brought me flowers when they arrived and my mom didn't hug me. Dad gave me a gentle kiss on the top of my head though.

"How are you feeling today?" Dad asked.

"Like I could run a marathon," I replied hoarsely.

"You sound like you've been smoking for ten years," Mom pointed out.

I turned my sunken, tired eyes to my perfectly made up mother.

"Thanks," I replied sarcastically. "That was exactly what I was going for."

"You don't need to be sarcastic about it," Mom said flatly. "I was merely pointing out that you should be getting better care in here and that there's no reason for you to sound like that."

"Yeah, sure," I said, rolling my eyes with a sigh. "They are honestly doing everything in their power, Mom. They're running tests, have me on super high-end painkillers and antibiotics. I feel weightless and you're complaining about my scratchy voice?"

I'd said just enough to push my mom's buttons.

"How dare you talk to me like that!" she exploded. "You are so rude, so selfish! Now that you're sick? You think you can take it out on me? No way, little girl. You're sick of your own accord, this is your problem, not mine and I will not have you spitting on my generosity, or the fact that I've come here to make sure you're all right."

"Maybe I don't need you here," I spat. I rolled over as much as I could, turning my back on my parents.

"Well then I'll just leave," Mom said huffily. I could hear her stand up, like she was really going to leave.

"Oh hush," Dad interjected. "Sit down, honey, you're not going anywhere."

I heard my mom drop huffily into her seat. I hid my smirk as best as I could. My mom was a drama queen at the best of times and this was going to be a very long day.

"Look," I said, rolling back over. "I'm sick."

"No shit," Mom sneered.

I bit my tongue to keep the snarky comeback away from her. I didn't need to fight with my mom, I really didn't have the strength for it.

"No, I mean, I'm really sick," I said. "I'm pretty sure that this is worse than a cold, or a lung infection."

Mom's face was carefully blank. Dad hung his head.

"What makes you think that?" Dad asked me.

I shrugged. "You don't keep someone in the hospital for a cold."

"And since when are you an expert?" Mom asked angrily. I knew then that she wasn't going to be civil with me. I had to take a deep breath to keep myself from having a fit and making things worse, but it was too late. I was already fed up with her attitude. I just wanted to go back to sleep.

"I'm sorry, Mom," I shot back, just as angrily. "You know what? Never mind. I was going to have a sincere heart to heart with you, to tell you that I'm sorry and that I love you and that I hope that you can still be proud of me, even though there is a good chance that I'm going to be a burden for the next little while they figure out what it is that is eating away at my insides, but you know what? Forget it." I was livid. I was shaking with anger, not just the weak shakes anymore.

My mom was hard to get along with already, I really didn't need her to fly off the handle at me, and make me fly off the handle to boot. It would make things more difficult, and we were technically in public. I didn't need to make a scene with my mom in public.

"Oh really?" Mom crooned in her angry diva voice. "You're sorry all of a sudden? You don't want to be a burden all of a sudden? You should have thought about everyone else's feelings and needs before you went gallivanting across the country to find a college willing to accept your grades, without even consulting me, no less! You don't know what you've managed to catch, and now you're in the hospital, being a baby about everything and getting angry at me for trying to care!"

"What?" I shouted, sending myself into a wild coughing fit.

"Calm down, you guys," Dad said quietly. "It's only been a few days since she's gotten worse, and she's only been in the hospital for one…"

"No!" Mom shouted over my coughing. I saw her get up out of the corner of my eye as I doubled over further and continued to cough out my lungs.

"No, this is unacceptable!" Mom was ranting. "Our daughter is sick. No one knows what's wrong, nothing is working and you want me to calm down?" Her face was flushed through the makeup she wore and she was gesticulating wildly as she shouted at my dad.

I reached for my water and sipped slowly to calm my coughing.

"Getting mad isn't going to help anyone," Dad said softly.

"Well obviously it's helping me!" Mom countered.

Dad sighed. "What do you want from me?" he asked my mom.

"I want you to find a doctor, drag his ass in here and start demanding answers!" Mom shrieked.

4

"Shall I just find any old doctor?" Dad asked sarcastically. "Or would you like the one specifically assigned to your daughter's case?"

"Well of course I would like the one specifically responsible for my daughter," Mom replied in her icy voice. We were both pushing her buttons and she was having none of it.

"Maybe you should go for a walk," Dad suggested. He was so calm and collected. I was amazed. I don't know how he had put up with my mom's insanity for so long, but now I was beginning to understand why they worked so well together.

My mom huffed a deep breath through her nose.

"Don't think that this is over," she snarled. She grabbed her purse and coat from the back of the chair and stormed out of my room, slamming the door as she went.

Dad sat down on the edge of the bed and smiled wanly at me.

"Sorry about that," he said sincerely. "I didn't want to bring her because she's been doing this all day."

"Really?" I asked.

"Yeah," Dad confirmed. He leaned back slightly, resting his huge hands on the bed. "At first, she didn't believe me. And last night when I told her everything, she started freaking out like that."

"Is she really mad?" I asked weakly.

Dad shrugged. "She blames everything and everyone for your illness," he offered. "She's mad that you went to look at schools and didn't take her. She's even angrier about the fact that you got sick at all. She's pissed off at the doctors for not sending you home faster. She's pissed off at the medicine for not fixing you. She's mad at the doctors here for not knowing what's actually wrong with you." He sighed. "The list goes on and on."

I nodded towards the door. My doctor was standing in the doorway, chart in hand. "Can I come in?" he asked.

"Of course," Dad said, standing. He offered his hand and the doctor took it. They shook hands warmly.

"Sorry to interrupt," Doctor Alexander was saying, "and I didn't mean to eavesdrop, but can I just say that your wife's reaction is completely normal?"

I laughed. "Normal?"

The doctor nodded. "Yes, we call it the five stages of grief. Many of our patients and their families go through the process when dealing with the onset of a severe or terminal illness."

"Terminal?" I croaked, applying the word to myself in my head. I must have sounded scared because my dad shot the doctor a look of warning.

"Not to say that you're terminal," Doctor Alexander added quickly. "I just mean, that um..." he stammered.

I smiled and waited for him to go on.

"I mean that it's normal in a sudden situation like this," he explained, trying to regain his composure. "When a family member is suddenly sick, and it seems too big." He shrugged. "It starts with denial, trying to convince ourselves that nothing is actually wrong, or that it isn't as bad as we think it is. Then anger, which we clearly just saw."

"Sorry about that," Dad said. "She's always been a bit of a firecracker."

Doctor Alexander smiled. "No worries," he said. "She stormed outside, muttering to herself about idiocy and new-age medical mumbo jumbo and HMOs."

"Definitely my wife," Dad said with a sigh.

"Aren't you glad I take after you?" I chimed in. "But with far better looks."

Dad laughed and I caught my doctor smiling at me.

"I deal with stress by being sarcastic," I pointed out.

"It's a lot more common than you'd think," the doctor replied easily, "I'm used to it."

"Guess I'll have to try harder then," I smirked.

"Guess you will," Doctor Alexander said.

I stopped for half a second, trying to wrap my fevered brain around that whole exchange. Part of me was hoping sincerely that I was correct and that he was flirting with me. Maybe the coffee date I had been fantasizing about was going to happen after all!

My dad cleared his throat, as though he had caught the flirtatious thoughts I was projecting and stole my doctor's attention.

"So this grief thing is normal?" he asked.

"Definitely," Doctor Alexander replied, "but everyone feels these things at different rates, some people take longer to process, some people act out differently." He smiled at my dad. "You seem to be coping quite well," he added. "Don't be surprised if you find yourself feeling relatively detached while your wife freaks out. That's also normal in a marriage. One person tends to be the stronger, silent type who lets everyone else lean on them while they grieve, and then you'll find yourself feeling these emotions later."

"Oh, okay," Dad said simply.

"Sorry to burst your macho bubble, Dad," I whispered.

"If you weren't so sick, I'd have to smack you around with a pillow," Dad warned.

I coughed a laugh. "Careful, Dad! Doctor Alexander might have to call child services."

"You're eighteen," my doctor interrupted. "It's an adult fight, I'd more likely have to call the cops."

My dad and I exchanged looks of disbelief and burst out laughing. My doctor was all right in our books. The merriment and general good feelings we were having were short lived however, as my mom returned just then.

"What's so damn funny?" she demanded. "I don't think that a sick child is anything to be laughing about."

"Neither is racism, but the jokes still exist and people still laugh at them," my doctor said calmly. He turned to face my mother and he held out his hand. "My name is Doctor Liam Alexander. I'm in charge of your daughter's case. It's a sincere pleasure to finally meet you. Your daughter is a wonderful patient."

"A wonderful patient?" my mom spat. She folded her arms across her chest.

Doctor Alexander looked at his hand in confusion and let it drop to his side. Dad groaned and I covered my face with my hand. We both knew what was coming.

"A wonderful patient in what way?" Mom demanded. "Because she's young and nubile? Because we have enough insurance to pay for whatever tests you feel like running today? Because she's quiet and doesn't complain about the terrible treatment she's getting from you people?"

"Terrible treatment?" Doctor Alexander repeated. "I'm sorry, what do you think qualifies as 'terrible treatment'?" he asked. "I'm here on my rounds on time, every time. I have six other cases, all as urgent as your daughter's and no less important."

"That's all fine and good," Mom said, quickly losing steam. She hadn't had an argument thought out and she wasn't prepared for Doctor Alexander to be so calm and collected in the face of her yelling. She was grasping at straws as she continued, "but there's no television in here, no nurses. No one has said word one to us about what is going on with our daughter!"

Doctor Alexander smiled. "For that, I apologize," he said sincerely. "You daughter requested a room with no television, if I recall correctly."

I nodded.

"As I thought," he continued, "there's nothing I can do about that particular issue. However, I'm sorry about the lack of information. I'm here now and I scheduled this visit to be at the end of my rounds so I have extra time to answer any questions you might have."

My mom was flabbergasted. She hadn't been expecting the doctor to be civil. Usually when she yelled and had a fit in public, she got her way, and usually it involved free or severely discounted things, meals, clothes, whatever she had her eye on at the moment. I'm positive that she hadn't been prepared for the doctor to be dealing for her in this manner.

"Right," Mom huffed instead. "Well, for starters, why is she alone all the time?"

"We have a busy hospital here, ma'am. We can't babysit," Doctor Alexander explained, shooting a glance in my direction and winking.

I grinned and felt a blush colour my cheeks.

"We are doing the absolute best that we can do to make sure that your daughter is treated. Currently we aren't sure what is making her sick We are running tests on the blood samples we took from her earlier and we are busily ruling out many diseases."

"Many?" Mom asked, her anger bubbling just below her surface.

"Yes," my doctor replied. "We have successfully ruled out, for the second time, AIDS, tuberculosis, cholera, typhoid and West Nile Virus. As well as Dengue fever and all forms of hepatitis."

"What are you currently testing for?" Dad asked suddenly.

"Currently we are running a full spectrum looking for things like cancer, lymphoma and leukemia," my doctor said calmly. "We're also running full diagnostics for liver, kidney, pancreatic, bladder and intestinal infections, as well as cancers of those organs." He smiled sincerely. "We are working as fast as we can to make sure that your daughter's condition will become known to us for sure and treatment will begin as soon as we have a better idea of what is making her ill."

"Well..." Mom stammered, looking for a reason to keep fighting. "What are you doing to treat her right now?"

"We have her on morphine to ease the pain --"

"You put my daughter on narcotics!" Mom asked, her voice rising. She was scandalized!

"Would you prefer something else?" Doctor Alexander asked. "And I can prescribe some Valium for you if you like?"

I stifled a snicker with a cough. Dad shot me a grin and Mom shook her head.

"Well I never!" Mom exclaimed. "Good day to you, Doctor," she said, the last word dripping with sarcasm and venom. She stormed back out of the room and stalked off.

"Oh thank God," I breathed. "I'm sorry, Doctor, she's a bit... overbearing sometimes."

My doctor waved it away. "Well, I'm glad that I could at least answer a few questions," he said with a smile. "Are you feeling all right?"

I shrugged. "About the same as before," I admitted. "Nauseous though."

He nodded. "That's the morphine and the antibiotics in you. It should pass soon," he assured me. "I'm hoping that the drugs will clear this up, and that you'll be right as rain in a couple days. I'll have someone bring you some more water, and some ginger ale for sure. And some broth. See if you can handle something a little more solid. You're not sleeping as much, so I think you could have something easy on your stomach, if you like?"

I nodded. "Sounds good."

Doctor Alexander smiled at me. "If there's nothing else, I'm gonna go check on the labs. I'll be back in a few hours."

"Thank you," I said sincerely. "You've been very helpful."

My doctor smiled and shook Dad's hand again before turning and leaving me alone with my dad.

"What?" I asked, catching the look my father was giving me.

"He's cute."

"Eew, Dad, don't say things like that, oh my God."

"What?" dad asked. "He's cute. Don't pretend like you didn't notice."

"Yeah, but for the love of everything holy, you can pretend that you didn't notice to spare me."

Dad laughed at me and tousled my hair. "I'm glad you noticed. He seems nice, and he wasn't too fazed by your mother. You have my blessings to bring him home."

I screwed up my face as Dad kissed the top of my head. "I'm gonna go find your mother and then try and get home. Do you want anything?"

"To have the last five minutes of my life back so we can not have the discussion about how cute my doctor is?"

"Anything realistic?"

I shook my head. "I just want to get better."

Dad nodded. "Yeah, I want that, too."

QUARANTINE

I had been in the hospital for a week since the fight with my mom when she exploded about me not having the care that she thought I deserved. Nothing new had happened. I was losing weight and unable to eat. All the soup and ginger ale I'd had? Thrown it all up. Doctor Alexander wasn't too thrilled by it, and to be honest, neither was I. They were adding new cocktails into the saline that was keeping me mostly hydrated, but I really missed food. Ginger ale wasn't too bad, and I mostly didn't throw up, but anything more than that and I was sick, either puking my guts out, or hobbling my weak ass to the bathroom for an hour. They stopped feeding me after that, and I spent a lot of my time sleeping. Unfortunately, my parents decided that they needed to spend as much time as they physically could with me in the hospitals, and when I wasn't sleeping I sat in awkward silence with my parents, or trying to make weak small talk.

I don't know how they could sit here with me all day. Mom usually went home and Dad would stay with me until the nurses came in to give me the night medications and sedate me into sleep. I suppose they had books or something with them when I was sleeping, but I never saw any evidence of what they actually got up to while they sat in the bleak hospital room with me.

There was no television in my room. I'd requested that I didn't have one, instead, I chose to have silence so that I could read, but I hadn't done much of that, either. My strength had begun to leave me even more than it had when I was first admitted. I found even holding small conversations with the doctors and with my parents had started to wear me out far quicker than I'd felt up until now. I sat quietly on the bed, wishing that I could read but I really just didn't have the strength. Mom had started reading a book aloud to me, but it wasn't the same, and I usually fell asleep after the first few sentences. I stared at my shaking hands and cursed the fact that I couldn't even read a book. My eyes filled with tears and I silently lamented the fact that I was sick.

My parents had gone to get coffee. I was alone again with my thoughts, which I was thankful for. Talking with my parents was trying and they never seemed to have anything new to say.

I was grateful to my parents, I didn't think that they would have stayed with me. They were still pretty much convinced that I wasn't as sick as the doctors were saying, and they both made sure that the doctors and nurses knew it. Even so, the familiar human contact was better than not having it at all. I hadn't seen my friends yet, though. Not since I was first admitted. I wondered if they were too afraid to come see me. Part of me worried that maybe I'd been contagious and I'd gotten one of them sick. The worry over infecting my best friend, her family or even her siblings, gnawed at my insides constantly. It was a sick feeling I'd been dealing with on top of the nausea and burning in my stomach from the sickness and the drugs. It sent a pang of sheer horror and sadness through me, knowing that my best friend in the whole world wasn't able to come see me.

I sighed to myself and fiddled with the edge of the thin blanket that covered me from the waist down. I stared at the device slipped over my finger and taped down so that I wouldn't accidentally pull it off. I had no idea what it was for. Part of me said that it was to monitor my oxygen intake, but that didn't seem right. I shook my head and let the thought go.

I yawned, then. Bored. My mom accidentally took my book with her when she and my father went to get coffee. Not that I could have really read it if I wanted to. Maybe I could get a television brought in or something. I didn't cope with boredom well. I shifted my weight to make myself more comfortable in the bed and I closed my eyes with a sigh.

I woke up with a start. I hadn't meant to fall asleep. I blinked and peered around the room blearily. My mom was sitting in her chair next to me, looking drawn, pallid and worried. My dad was standing near the window of the room, staring out at some doctors, but I couldn't tell if they were the doctors who had been in to see me or not.

I smacked my lips, my mouth felt like it had been stuffed with cotton.

"What's going on?" I asked hoarsely.

My mom started. She hadn't noticed I'd woken up. I wondered vaguely how long I'd been asleep. The coffee they'd gotten stood on the little table, I could smell it, but it had been long forgotten by my parents.

"Nothing, sweetie," Mom said quietly.

"You're lying to me," I accused weakly, a smirk trying to play against my lips, with little success. I was tired.

My mom smiled tiredly. She poured a glass of water from the pitcher on the table and put my straw in it. She held it out to me and I sipped the water greedily. "Not too fast, honey," she warned.

I obeyed.

"Nothing is happening," Mom continued. "No one has been in to see you since this morning."

"What time is it?" I asked, my voice sounding more normal to me now that I'd had a drink.

"Three thirty."

I'd been asleep for more than three hours! I glared at the IV line dripping steadily into my arm and cursed the doctor who drugged me with sleeping medication. If I wanted sleep, I would sleep. I didn't need drug-induced rest during the day. The drugs at night, however, were a different story.

"So really, nothing's happening?" I asked. Something didn't feel quite right. Mom wouldn't look so worried if there wasn't something happening. I was just sick. That was all. The hospital was just being safe.

Mom sighed. "No," she said, forcing a smile, "nothing's happening." She patted my hand gently. "How are you feeling?"

I shrugged weakly. "Tired," I admitted, "kind of weak." I looked her over. "You look exhausted, mom. Are you getting any sleep at all?"

Mom smiled again. "We go home at night," she said, "after they give you your medication. You doze right off, and we go home, then I take a shower and try to sleep. It really depends on the night."

"Go home?" I suggested. "Take a day off and get some rest. Go to the zoo or something." I smiled bravely. "I'll be fine for a day alone," I promised. "Maybe I'll get some sleep and it'll help speed up my recovery."

"That's a great idea," Dad said. He didn't turn from his spot staring at the doctors in the hallway. "You stay home tomorrow, honey. I'll stay here."

15

I strained my eyes to make out the doctors outside the window. I couldn't tell who they were, if they were my doctors or not. They seemed to be going through some thick piles of paperwork and looking at something in a binder. I wondered if they were my doctors going through my charts or something.

"No!" Mom argued, "I can't leave my daughter in the hospital!"

"Mom," I gently placed my hand on top of hers. "I'll be all right here by myself for a day. And Dad can stay with me if you guys are really that worried about me being alone. I'm not picky."

Dad snickered under his breath. I don't think he was expecting me to make the argument for my mom to go. He was usually the one to kick Mom out of places that she shouldn't be. I just didn't want to argue anymore. We both knew that a lot of the time my mom could be the cause of a lot of stress and insanity. She'd also been very vocal about exactly what she thought about the treatment I'd been receiving thus far.

My mom sighed loudly and nodded. "You're probably right," she agreed. "You always were a very thoughtful and considerate young lady."

"Thanks Mom," I replied with a smile. If she was being sarcastic, I didn't notice.

"Those doctors sure do a whole hell of a lot of nothing," Dad muttered.

"What do you mean?" I asked. "I think they've done a fantastic job caring for me so far."

Dad laughed mirthlessly. "They still haven't come up with a reason why you're sick," he pointed out.

I shrugged. "Maybe it's just a really bad flu, like I've been saying this whole time."

"Maybe it's something worse," Dad countered.

"You know, your paranoid attitude doesn't help me feel any better," I said. "I'm the one who is sick here. You and Mom always talking about how much worse this sickness might be really doesn't make me want to get better. It scares me!"

Dad sighed, letting his shoulders slump. He was more tired than I thought.

Quietly, my dad crossed the room and sat on the edge of my bed. He wrapped his huge arms around my shoulders. I could feel his whiskers tickling my neck and cheek as he held me close. His breath was warm against my skin. It felt good to have that little bit of human contact. I hadn't gotten a hug since the day I got sick.

"I'm sorry," Dad said quietly. "I'm just still so angry that these guys are taking all this money and all this time and they still haven't figured out what's wrong with you. It's not fair. It's not right. We pay these guys so much in salaries and they stand around talking, doing nothing. I've been watching them for an hour at least."

"Are they even my doctors?" I asked.

"Yes," Dad replied. "They've been looking through some books or something for like forty-five minutes."

"I'm sure that they have other patients," I pointed out as Dad finally let me go. "Maybe they're referencing someone else's case or something."

"I have a really bad feeling about this," Dad warned. "They spend all this time looking in books instead of fixing you. What are we paying them for?"

"Dad! Chill out!" I exclaimed, sending myself into a coughing fit.

Dad patted my back gently as I struggled to stop coughing. I took a sip of the water through the straw.

"I'm sure that they are doing everything that they can to keep me alive. I'm a new case, a new situation that no one has seen before. I'm not gonna complain if they want to cross-reference other cases and other charts in between visiting me and doing their rounds. I can wait, and I would rather know that they are positive that what I have isn't something contagious before they send me home."

Dad nodded and patted my shoulder again. "You're such a trooper."

I snorted. "Naw, I'm just stubborn and I get it from you," I replied with a smirk.

Dad tousled my hair affectionately. "It's true!" he agreed.

Even Mom laughed at that. It was nice, we were like a family again.

But even the nicest illusions can be stripped away.

The door opened and the doctor my dad had been watching stood in the door. He had a mask over his face and he refused to come further into the room. It wasn't Liam, I didn't know who this doctor was. I hoped he was important, and that my dad tore his face off. There was something unnerving about the whole thing.

"I'm sorry to interrupt," he said. "But I am afraid that we will be moving your daughter into quarantine in fifteen minutes."

My parents exchanged a panicked look. Dad was on his feet instantly, as if he was about to fight the doctor to keep him from taking me away. Mom placed her hand against her mouth and I could see tears of fear in her eyes. The electrodes on my chest sent their signals to the monitor and everyone knew instantly that my heart rate had spiked. No one said anything about it, thankfully.

"Quarantine?" my mom asked shrilly. "What do you mean by that?"

"We mean," the doctor said calmly, "that we are going to be moving her to a special wing where there will be no chance of this infection spreading to other patients."

"You think I'm contagious?" I asked incredulously.

"Do you know what is making my daughter sick?" Dad demanded.

"Not exactly," the doctor said.

"What does that mean?" Dad pressed. "Not exactly? Either you know, or you don't!"

"We don't know," the doctor said with a sigh. "We are placing your daughter in quarantine to make sure that whatever is causing this illness doesn't spread any further."

"You think it's communicable?" I asked.

"We don't know," the doctor said again. "So far all of our tests are coming up abnormal compared to what we would expect. We've run tests to rule out cancer, AIDS, tuberculosis. The whole spectrum, really. We have no idea what's causing this and we want to put you in quarantine for your own safety."

"My own safety?" I echoed.

"That and the safety of our staff and other patients," the doctor corrected himself quickly. "Your parents will be put into overnight quarantine and we will run a few tests on them just to make sure that they haven't contracted this already."

"Okay," I said with a smile.

"No!" my dad bellowed. "You can't just come in here, tell me that my daughter is sick with something, that you don't know what it is and then tell me that she's being quarantined like a rabid dog!" he shouted. His face was turning red as he yelled at the poor doctor. I felt kind of sorry for the guy; he hadn't known that my dad was such a scary man when he was angry.

"You are not taking my daughter to a secret facility to test her until she's dead," Dad continued rambling. "She is my daughter and I refuse to allow this!"

"I'm really sorry, but you don't have that right," the doctor replied. "She's over eighteen, and it is protocol for us to quarantine her due to the nature of her illness. Now we can do this civilly and quietly, or we can sedate you as well and drag you to your overnight quarantine on a gurney. It's up to you."

My mom burst out crying just then. She always did have an excellent mind for dramatic timing. My dad was fuming, I swear I could see smoke rising from his head. It was comical, really. My huge, muscular, unshaven father and my frail, made-up, dressed up mother. The doctor looked like he wasn't sure what was happening. He was like a deer caught in the headlights. It was all I could do not to laugh aloud at the silliness of the entire situation.

Dad wrapped his arms around my mom, who was still sobbing and mumbling nonsensically into her hands. He patted her shoulder gently with his huge hand.

"Give us a minute." He growled warningly at the doctor.

The young doctor nodded and closed the door.

I burst out laughing. Mom and Dad both gave me a look that suggested that I was insane. I didn't care. It was too hilarious.

"You scared the crap out of him," I said, wheezing.

Dad smiled. "Damn right I did," he replied proudly. "No one takes me daughter away to quarantine without a damn good explanation."

"Why were you so eager to go to the quarantine with him?" Mom asked through her sobs, dabbing at the running mascara on her face. "You know that you'll die in there."

"Mom, you're so melodramatic," I said quietly. "If it's their protocol, there's nothing that you can do about it. There's no point in arguing. Besides, I couldn't live with myself if I found out that this illness or whatever I have spread to all the doctors and nurses who've been in here. Could you imagine what sort of scandal that would be?"

Mom and Dad exchanged worried looks again.

"Besides," I pressed. "Wouldn't you rather be famous for being the parents of the girl who saved the world than for being the parents of the girl who started an incurable pandemic in Saint Thomas' hospital?"

Mom and Dad were very quiet. It was like they had to consider the options that I'd presented to them.

"Plus, you don't wanna go home and spread this," I pointed out. "Wouldn't you rather know that you're both clean and healthy and not carriers of this too?"

Mom began to sob hysterically again. Dad pulled her close against his hip.

"How can you be so clever when you're so sick?" Dad asked me.

"I have..." I mumbled, suddenly exhausted. "I have... really really good genetics..."

My head began to droop. I felt myself nodding.

Oh my God, I thought. *What the hell is this?* But it was too late. My head dropped forward, once, twice, three times. I felt the cup of water slip from my fingers and clatter to the floor. I slumped forward as sleep took over my body, except that it wasn't exactly sleep. It was more like a sudden unconsciousness. I felt my temperature spike. My whole body flopped backwards and began to convulse violently.

The beeping machines in the room went insane, chirping wildly and beeping loudly as my body jumped and twitched against the bed.

I heard my mother scream.

My dad pulled open the door and began shouting for someone to help.

I could feel the hands pressed against my body. My saliva foamed at the corners of my mouth and my teeth clattered together as the convulsions wracked my body harder against the bed. I could see everything going on around me until my eyes rolled back in my head.

The voices around me blended into a cacophony of white noise and my body was covered in sweat. My knees and elbows locked up as the shakes continued. God, did it ever hurt. My muscles strained inside my flesh, pressing against the bones and skin, fighting to shake my body harder against the hands and arms that pressed against me.

Someone grabbed my face to keep my head from shaking too much. My neck strained hard against them and I hoped that I would just break my neck and end this suffering. I wanted to scream, but even my vocal cords were tight and useless.

Finally, a needle was stabbed into the taught flesh of my arm and the muscles there went suddenly limp. My body slowed from the violent, possessed shakes and I felt a different kind of drowsiness come over me.

They had sedated me, I think.

I could hear my mom babbling and sobbing over top of the shouted gibberish that was medical lingo. My eyes searched the room, not seeing anything.

I heard my name.

"Can you hear me?"

I tried to respond, but my words came out in a choking, high pitched wheezing kind of noise.

A new beeping kind of noise started up in my ears.

"She can't breathe!" someone shouted.

Even through the muscle relaxants and sedatives they'd just pumped me full of I could feel the tube sliding down my throat. I wanted to gag, to throw up, to pull it out of my throat, but I couldn't.

The last thing I heard as the sedatives kicked in fully was, "We're taking her to quarantine."

Pathogen: Patient Zero

BARGAINING

When I woke up, I was in a different room than the one I had previously been in. The walls here were all stark white. I peered around the place, it was like I was looking at everything through a film. Or a bubble. I didn't understand where I was. My brain felt all fuzzy and addled from the sedation.

I smacked my lips. I was thirsty.

"Hello?" I called as loudly as I could. My voice was muffled to my own ears, I didn't understand it. I was uncomfortable and alone. It was a stark contrast to where I had been before.

"Hello?" I mumbled again.

A hissing noise caught my attention. There was a door and it was automated, like at a shopping center or grocery store. It was shiny metal and it slid open with a hiss. I blinked and whimpered in fear as a white-suited figure approached me. The suit looked like it was made out of paper and I couldn't see the face of the person who was approaching because they were wearing a mask and safety goggles.

"What?" I whispered, panicking.

It was then that I realized that I couldn't move my hands or feet.

The beeping heart monitor began chirping loudly as my heart rate jumped. I was terrified. I didn't know where I was, I didn't know what was happening and I didn't know how long I had been asleep.

The white-clad figure hurried over to me, hands held up in a placating manner.

"Shh! It's okay! It's okay!" he said.

I watched as he pulled against something, a zipper I deduced from the noise it made as he pulled, and he stepped through the film that made everything look like I was in a bubble. He stepped up to the bed and placed a hand against my shoulder.

"Hey, calm down," he told me. "It's me, Doctor Alexander."

I blinked stupidly. I felt like a moron. Of course I was still in the hospital.

"Where am I?" I asked weakly.

"You're in the quarantine room we set up for you," the doctor explained. "You've been unconscious for about thirty hours."

"Where are my parents?" I asked.

"They went home to sleep," Doctor Alexander said gently. "They were tested and held in quarantine for a day to make sure that they weren't sick."

"And they're all right?" I asked.

"Very much so," he replied. "They've gone home to get some sleep and they'll be back to visit you."

I breathed a sigh of relief. "Why can't I move?"

"Your arms and legs are strapped down," the doctor explained. I couldn't see his face, just his dark eyes. I seemed to recall that he was really cute. "You had a severe seizure and we sedated you before we brought you here."

"Have I had more?"

Doctor Alexander shook his head. "Not since we sedated you. The straps were just a precaution."

I arched an eyebrow. "Couldn't I have broken something if I'd seized?"

He regarded me with a blank stare, even though I couldn't see his face under the mask.

"I'll stop asking questions," I offered.

He nodded. "Anything I can get for you?"

"I need a drink," I whispered. "And to be untied," I asked, "please?"

Doctor Alexander nodded. He removed the straps from my wrists and ankles first and I breathed a sigh of relief. I watched him as he poured me a glass of water in the familiar pink plastic tumblers of Saint Thomas' hospital. He placed a bendy straw in it for me and held it out.

Without thinking, a leaned forward to take a sip only to be blocked by the oxygen mask that I didn't realize was over my mouth. No wonder my voice sounded muffled and weird.

Doctor Alexander tried to stifle his laugh and I smiled dozily at him. I was drugged out of my mind and sleepy, I'd been unconscious for a day and a half and I didn't know the damn thing was there. I sighed and allowed him to lift the mask from my face.

"Thank you," I said sincerely as the straw met my lips. The water was cool and wonderful against my parched and sore throat. My whole body ached; I wondered if it was from the convulsions I had the day before.

I felt a choking sob well up in my throat. I began to cough and I did a spit-take of water all over my blanket and Doctor Alexander's white paper hazmat suit.

"Oh gosh, I'm sorry," I said, choking and weakly trying to sit up.

"Don't worry about it," Doctor Alexander said with a shake of his head. He pressed a button on the side of my bed and the whole thing began to move. It pulled me into a sitting position and I felt the coughing begin to subside.

"Much better," I assured him. "Thank you."

"No worries," he replied.

He regarded me for a long moment, holding the plastic cup in one hand. I wished that he wasn't wearing a mask, I would have liked to see his face again, and maybe I would have understood the look he was giving me a little better if he hadn't been wearing the mask.

"What's wrong?" I asked suddenly very self-conscious.

"Your eyes are..." He trailed off.

"What's wrong with my eyes?" I asked, lifting one hand to my face.

"The seizure..." he began slowly, turning his eyes away from me and setting the cup back down on the familiar bedside table that was standard for hospital rooms. "It burst the blood vessels in your eyes," he explained.

"What does that mean?" I asked, frowning.

"It just means that the whites of your eyes are all blood red," he told me. "It brings out the colour of your irises in a way that is mildly unsettling, and strangely pretty at the same time."

I blinked and let my hand fall against my lap.

"Why, Doctor," I said with a smirk, "if I didn't know better, I would think that you were hitting on me."

He laughed nervously. "No. Just complimenting your eyes," he replied. "And worrying that I might be turning into a hemophiliac."

It was my turn to snort a laugh. "It's like three in the morning isn't it?" I asked. "And you've worked a double to make sure that I'm okay, haven't you?"

"How could you tell?" he asked.

I smiled faintly, suddenly weak and tired. "It's all right," I assured him gently, yawning openly as I was too weak and tired to hide it. "I appreciate the work you've put in and I won't tell anyone."

His eyes smiled at me. "You're a sweetheart," he said, placing his gloved hand against my swollen and taped one. "I'm going to do everything in my power to find a cure for you."

"Thanks," I said sleepily. "Will my parents be allowed to see me later?"

"Definitely," he assured me. "I mean, as long as you want them to?"

"Ha ha, you try and keep them out of here," I said. "You remember what my mom was like when she wasn't convinced that you were doing anything good for me? Now multiply that by a hundred and you'll get an idea of what she'd be like if you didn't let her come into the quarantine room because of whatever reason you'd have to give her."

Doctor Alexander's face crinkled, and the mask and suit made a pleasant rustling noise as I assumed he made a face of horror at the thought of my mother's wrath. "Yes, we will be allowing them to visit as long as they follow the rules."

I smiled and nodded my agreement. "Okay," I replied with another yawn. "I'm gonna sleep some more," I told him as my eyes began to close.

"Sleep well."

I heard him adjust the drip on my IV lines, the machine making a soothing beeping noise. Then, there was the rustle of the paper suit and the plastic tarp followed by the pull of the zipper and I was alone to sleep.

I woke with a start. One of my machines was beeping. I don't know which one, but there was a burning sensation in my hand.

"Nurse?" I whispered, my throat too sore from the strain on my vocal cords the seizures had caused.

"Just changing your IV, dear," she said. I let my head drop to the side, I was still sitting up. There was definitely a nurse in my room, inside the tarp and dressed in a yellow paper suit. I blinked in the light, my eyes not pleased by the harshness of the light today.

"Are my parents here?" I asked.

"They are just being briefed," she replied primly. She didn't even look at me. I wondered if my eyes were really that off-putting. Doctor Alexander had said that they were filled with blood instead of being normal and white.

Doctor Alexander also said that he was gonna do everything that he could to fix me. I wondered when I would get to see him. The charismatic doctor made me feel a lot better about the entire situation.

The nurse left without another word.

I muttered a few not terribly nice things about her as she left and immediately felt bad. My mom's anger from the other day seemed to have infected me suddenly. I sighed and placed my hand against the oxygen mask against my face. The weight of it was strangely comforting. I wondered if I huffed it enough, could I get high like I'd heard, or was that a rumour?

I pushed those thoughts out of my mind, decided that hyperventilating while trying to get high on oxygen might not be the smartest thing to do. I laughed to myself and closed my eyes while I waited for my parents.

I'm not sure if I fell asleep or not, but the burning in my hand where the IV was connected to me snapped me to attention. There were a few white-clad hazmat suits hanging around outside of the film. I couldn't tell if they were talking or not, the beeping of my heart monitor kept their voices from reaching me. I breathed deeply and tried to mentally prepare myself for bad news. The body language of the hazmat suits suggested that something unpleasant was happening. The zipper sounded, the metallic pulling noise was harsh and unpleasant to my ears. I winced and tried to sit up further, no avail.

Two of the suits walked forward.

"How are you holding up, honey?" It was my dad.

I breathed a sigh of relief.

"I'm all right," I said. "I've been sleeping a lot."

"You look awful," Mom said.

"Thanks," I replied. "I haven't been in for my facial yet."

Mom shook her head. "We are so worried about you. Everyone is."

"I could only imagine," I replied more sarcastically than I intended.

"You don't have to be rude," Mom snapped.

"Sorry," I acquiesced. "I'm really scared right now."

"Are you?" Dad asked.

"Scared?" I asked. "Yes."

"Why didn't you say something before, then? We would have come back sooner, or fought harder to stay with you."

I shrugged as best as I could. I felt like all my strength had been sapped out of me. "It's hard to explain," I said, lamely. "I mean, I could feel everything when I had that seizure," I explained. "They put a tube down my throat at some point? I could feel that even though I wasn't really awake."

"Did you tell your doctor that?" Dad asked.

"No," I said shaking my head. "I didn't think that it was very important."

"I think everything that you can tell the doctors about how you feel is important at this point," Dad told me. "If you think there's anything that they should know, you should tell them." He sighed and ran a hand though his hair. I could see that he was stressing out almost as much as mom was at

30

this point. "It might allow them to treat your condition better, you know. You might get outta here faster."

I nodded. "Okay, if I can think of anything, I'll tell Doctor Alexander when he comes back to see me."

"Have you seen him at all today?" Mom asked.

"Not since three in the morning," I admitted. "He was working a double. He said I'd been unconscious for thirty hours after my seizure," I explained. "It's... it's still the same day, right? I mean, I had that seizure yesterday and have only been in quarantine for a day?"

Dad nodded. "Yeah. We got some rest in those thirty hours, we were in quarantine overnight, and then we went home, showered, changed, had a bite to eat, and came to see you."

"This time jumping and losing hours because I'm unconscious thing is really freaky," I said, shaking as a coughing fit started to shake my body.

"You look horrible," Mom reiterated. "You've lost another five pounds, easily. Aren't they feeding you in here?"

"I've been unconscious, Mom," I wheezed. "I'm pretty sure that they're nourishing me through the IV lines, though. Besides, every time I try to eat anything I get sick. You know this. The IV vitamins and stuff is all I can handle, so they're keeping me fed, in a way."

"It's not the same," Mom argued. "You need some good, home cooked food. I'll bring you something to eat tonight at suppertime, okay? It'll make you feel much better to get some home cooking into your tummy. It'll have you fixed right up."

"Mom, I dunno if that's allowed," I said slowly, "but I appreciate the thought." I smiled behind my oxygen mask. "You might wanna bring Doctor Alexander something though, he needs it more than I do, and he's taking such good care of me."

31

Mom nodded vaguely, but didn't say anything. I still don't think she ever forgave Doctor Alexander for arguing with her the first time.

I stared at my parents though the white paper suits they wore. They both had protective goggles and surgical masks on, and even their hands were covered with the blue latex gloves that all the doctors wore here. I noticed a bulge beneath Mom's suit at her neckline.

"Are you wearing your rosary?" I asked my mom.

"Yes," Mom replied and I noticed the tears welling up in her eyes. "Is that so wrong?"

My mom only wore her rosary when she was desperate. When she needed a sale, she wore it. When she was praying for news, she wore it. She took it with her on business trips and the held it tightly when I had my wisdom teeth out.

"Mom... are you... are you trying to like... bargain with God?"

"I have been praying," Mom shot back defensively. "The whole church is praying for a speedy recovery for you."

I blinked rapidly. "Oh, okay. Thank you," I said stupidly. I didn't know what else to say. I was sick in the hospital, and my mom was busily bargaining with the God she only believed in on Sundays or when she needed something marginally divine in nature.

I felt like my head was about to explode.

"Tell you what, kiddo," Dad interjected before I could go on a rant. "You kick this thing in the ass, get better and get outta this plastic tent of yours, and when you're feeling stronger, we'll go on a nice family vacation. Maui, or Disneyland or something. Hell, we can go to Europe, check out Oxford? Maybe see if you've got enough credentials to get in?"

"Are you trying to bribe my body into getting better?" I asked.

"Should I offer it a spa day and ice cream, too?" Dad asked me.

I would have laughed if it wasn't quite so sad. I nodded.

"Deal," Dad said.

The zipper opened just then and a new masked face poked inside the sanctuary of my plastic fumigation tent. "I'm sorry folks, but you'll have to leave now. The doctor will be here momentarily and there are a few tests we need to run on your daughter."

It was the same nurse who had refused to look me in the eye, I was sure of it.

"Can't we just have a few more minutes?" Mom asked. "I'm sure the tests can wait for ten more minutes. We might not be able to come back today."

"I'm sorry, ma'am, but there are other people waiting to use the labs, we need to get the tests into the labs as quickly as possible."

"Mom, Dad, it's all right," I said quietly. "I'll be all right. You guys can come see me tomorrow. Everything will be fine, I'm in good hands here," I said, trying to reassure them. I knew that I shouldn't have admitted to being scared. That was dumb of me, but they had the right to know how terrified I was, didn't they? They were being strong for my benefit; I had the right to lean on my parents, didn't I?

Mom nodded and blinked back her tears. She leaned over and kissed my forehead through her paper surgical mask. "We'll come see you as soon as possible."

"And don't forget to bring Doctor Alexander a cake or some dinner or something, Mom," I reminded her. "Make sure he gives me extra special good care that way."

Dad chuckled. "You're a spunky little thing," he told me gently. "I love you, kiddo and I'm really proud of you."

"Thanks, Dad," I replied. "It means a lot. I'll be sure to kick this thing's ass and go on making you proud later."

Dad tousled my sweaty, matted hair and tried not to wince.

I smiled and waggled my fingers weakly in an attempt to say goodbye.

I watched sadly with my bloody eyes as my parents were escorted out of the room. The metal, automated door opened with a hiss and a swooshing noise and the figures of my parents disappeared beyond it.

I really hoped that God was listening to my mom, and for that matter, the rest of the church. I was already beginning to doubt the sincerity of the statement claiming that there was an entire congregation praying for me, but it was the thought that counted, right? Mom was trying to make me feel better, after all. I sighed and leaned back against the thin pillow. It wasn't very comfortable, but it was all I had. The burning in my hand persisted as I waited for the doctor to arrive.

"All right," I said quietly. "I'm sick, that much is obvious. I have an unidentifiable disease and they are going to do tests on me to figure it out." I looked at my body, hidden underneath the thin blanket and the thinner hospital gown.

"Body, you have to listen to me. You're not in charge here. I am. Me, the one who inhabits you. I'm not ready to become a medical case number. And I'm sure as hell not ready to become a case study or an example to students. So you're gonna get over this sickness. I don't care what it is or what you have to do to get rid of it. We're not going down without a fight.

"This quarantine thing? I'm not happy with it, and there's no way that you can be either. We're young, still, body. We're only eighteen. We haven't even learned how to drive yet. We're still single, too. Don't you wanna write a novel? Don't you wanna go learn karate? And what about Disneyland?"

I balled up my fists in anger.

"Dammit!" I swore. "This is stupid. You're stronger than this, body, you hear me? You didn't work your ass off with me to keep our grades up for this! You didn't help me get through those torturous years of living in my crazy mother's house just to wind up sick with the dengue fever in the hospital at eighteen! I'm stronger than this! We're stronger than this!"

I suddenly shivered. A chill swept through me and set my teeth chattering against themselves. "This is ridiculous!" I croaked. "I'm better than this!" I stared at the burning spot on my hand where the IV line was taped to my skin. I could see the veins beneath my skin sticking out. It was itchy and burning and annoying as hell.

"I have had enough of hospitals!" I decided. "And you're not letting me go down in here, body!"

My first move was to take the oxygen mask away from my face. I pulled it over my head, but it took me moment to get it over my ponytail. It was all tangled up in my hair and I whimpered as I struggled with my left hand to get it out. My right hand was useless with the IV taped to it and I couldn't lift it past my elbow without feeling the pull of the tape and the needle moving about under my skin. The thought of that alone sent my stomach rolling in disgust and fear. Working with my off hand, it took me longer than I thought it would, but I was soon free from the mask.

I sat in my bed silently, breathing heavily. I'd been drugged and unconscious off and on for a week, my strength had been sapped by the sickness that was busily ravaging my body. I stared at the oxygen mask in my hand and considered taking a few more hits from it until I caught my breath.

"No," I told myself, tossing the mask to the floor on the far side of my bed. "If I wanna get out, I have to get out entirely."

With strengthening resolve, I forced my left hand to grasp the tape and IV line on my right. I was so weak, but I was determined not to stay in this hospital bed any longer. Picking at it in a highly uncoordinated manner, I peeled the clear tape away from my flesh. My skin had thinned out considerably and the tape peeling away tore part of my flesh away, leaving a scrape-like square of exposed skin. I swore heavily under my breath. I hated scrapes worse than anything and that's what the tape burn felt like. I watched a small drop of blood bubble up against my pale skin and almost threw up.

With another desperate swear word under my breath, I pulled the IV line out of my arm, stifling a scream of pain by biting my lip. Blood spurted up, mingling with the tea-coloured liquid that had moments ago been pumping into my body.

I stared at the needle and the IV line, dripping with whatever sort of medicine was supposed to be dripping into my veins. It glistened in the harsh light of my room and shone slightly red with my blood. I cast it aside, tossing it haphazardly to the floor. I spotted the glass of water on the table and I grabbed it, gulping it down greedily.

I let the cup clatter to the floor, dropping it from my fingers like a bit of refuse that I no longer cared about and I staggered forward toward the zipper in the fumigation tent that surrounded me and separated me from the rest of the room.

I swayed unsteadily on my feet, not sure if it was the sickness in me or the drugs that was making me so unsteady. I fumbled against the thick plastic, momentarily worried that I was going to crash right through it if I fell over. I was dizzy and weak and it was making this far more complicated than it ought to be.

My breath was wheezing in my chest, I was finding it hard to breathe. Apparently, I had needed that oxygen mask after all.

I placed my hand against the plastic of the tent thing that covered my immediate area. I was surprised to find it thick and sturdy enough to hold at least a little bit of weight if I pressed against it. My hand slipped a little as I swayed, trying to maintain my balance. I reached up above my head to grasp the thick zipper that would let me out. My fingers were shaking and I wasn't able to grasp the zipper on the first try.

It took me three tries to grab the zipper and it took more than one pull to bring it down.

I felt a small rush of air as the zipper created the aperture through which I meant to escape. I leaned heavily against the thick plastic, allowing myself a moment to breathe the air that was flowing around the outside of the tent. It wasn't much, but it was circulated within the room and it felt air conditioned. It was a pleasant feeling.

Weakly, I pulled against the zipper some more, pulling it down as far as I could. I moved to lean over to pull it open all the way, but nearly fell onto my face. I whimpered quietly to myself. If I fell, it wouldn't be pretty. I stopped then, holding tightly on to the edge of the hole in the tent. My knuckles were white and the wound on my hand from the tape and the needle dripped blood that seeped up through my skin and landed on the floor or smeared across the plastic whenever I moved. It didn't register in my mind that the familiar red in my blood was quickly being replaced by an abnormal brownish colour.

I took a moment to regain my strength and pulled one last time on the zipper. The opening was at my knees now.

"Good enough," I mumbled.

Carefully, I climbed through the doorway I'd created, gripping the rough edges of the opening tightly. I lifted my right leg first, holding fast to the zippered edge, ignoring where it dug into the thin flesh of my palms. I set my bare foot down carefully on the floor on the outside of the fumigation tent and paused to get my breath.

I sent a longing glance towards the bed, wishing that I hadn't thrown the oxygen mask so far away now. I shook my head gently, to keep the dizziness from overwhelming me, and I stood as still as I could, half in the tent, half out and holding onto the edge of it for dear life.

When the spinning slowed down to a manageable speed, I lifted my other leg through the hole in the tent. I stared at the bed where I had been moments ago with a look of utter contempt.

"Good riddance," I growled, though I didn't realize that it was more of a guttural growl than actual words.

Carefully, I made my way away from the tent. I found myself staring at this quarantine room for the first time without the film of the tent obscuring my view.

The room was white, like I had known, but it was far larger than I had originally thought. The lights were buzzing fluorescent bulbs that showered everything in a harsh white light and gave the room an entirely unwelcome sci-fi feeling. It was like something out of countless alien books and movies. I felt like I wasn't even on earth anymore, it was so surreal and I didn't want to think about the possibility that they were going to do actual experiments on me. I felt suddenly nauseous as I stared at the instruments and machinery that had been surrounding me the whole time. There were things that looked like medieval torture devices, monitors for God only knew what, a machine that I knew was a defibrillator and about a thousand small tools that I didn't want to even hazard a guess at.

A shudder shook my body. What had they been planning to do to me? My mind wandered to all sorts of horrific things, spurred on by the thought that I wasn't quite on earth, maybe I'd been moved to Area 51 or something? I doubled over and vomited. My body retched as thick, dark vomit splattered against the stark white floor.

A panic alarm went off in my mind and I realized that I hadn't eaten anything for at least three days, what was I throwing up?

I stared at the brownish puddle on the floor and wiped my mouth with the back of my left hand. I stared about the room again, swaying on the spot. My eyes landed on the silver tray of hand tools, one of which I recognized as a scalpel. Another one of the tools, I knew, was a pair of forceps.

Overcome suddenly by a fit of rage, I flipped the tray with the tools, sending them clattering to the ground with the tinkling sound of metal against metal.

I screamed in impotent rage and pushed one of the machines. I barely moved it in my weakened state and that seemed to fuel my anger even further. I looked at the tools on the ground and picked up the scalpel. I stared at it for a long moment before rushing at the fumigation tent that had surrounded me. I slashed mindlessly at the plastic, stabbing holes in it and making long tears where I could. I felt hot tears pouring down my face as I growled and screamed at the plastic.

Fed up with the lack of utter destruction, I cast aside the scalpel, sending it skittering across the floor somewhere where I couldn't see it. It was probably for the best. I wanted to destroy something, to hurt things. I couldn't control myself.

I picked up the tray that had held the tools themselves and swung it feebly at one of the machines with a screen. I screamed again and swung a second time. I was a mess, a feeble, weak mess and there was nothing that I wanted to do more in that moment than destroy everything in that room. I wanted to get out of there. I wanted to go home. I wanted this place to hurt.

I swung the tray at the screen a few more times, trying desperately to break it, with no luck. I threw the tray a pathetic distance away from me in my dismay and growled again.

There was an observation window near the door. I wondered if the door would open. I hobbled across the room, drooling slightly in my rabid fit of anger. My red-tinged eyes swept around the room. I stopped at the door, waiting for it to open.

It didn't open.

"Open!" I told it. It didn't move. "OPEN!" I screamed at it.

The door stood apathetic and stoic against my screaming demands.

Frustrated, I began to pound against it, screaming at it to open and to let me out. When that didn't work, I felt my knees buckle weakly. I leaned into the door, sobbing with rage and dismay and I sank to the floor.

"Open..." I begged, sobbing about my own inability to let myself out. The pathetic sadness soon made way for a new bubbling anger towards myself.

I didn't realize what I was doing until I had my fingers firmly wrapped in my hair and was pulling handfuls of it out. I sat there, ripping chunks of my hair out and screaming in pain, tears rolling freely down my cheeks. I noticed the wound on my hand and began picking at it, widening the already bleeding tear. I was detached from myself, like I was watching someone else do these horrible things in my body. I couldn't stop myself and I couldn't control myself. I just sat there, picking at the open wound. The strange brown colour of the flowing blood didn't even register with me.

As I sat, gouging my hand with my nails, I began to nod and my temperature rose. I nodded a steady rhythm and fell asleep against the door.

"Jesus Christ."

The swear, breathed in loud horror brought me to consciousness. I began coughing, my body shaking with the force of it.

"I need help in here!" It was my doctor. It was Liam, I knew that voice at least. He was yelling as I shook on the floor, choking and gasping for air.

"Oh my God..." I begged through the coughing. "Help me..."

I was in pain. There was so much pain. I had never felt anything like it in my life. Every inch of my body hurt. I didn't know where I was, I felt the cold floor beneath me. I felt the pain in my hand, and in my head. I was sore, like I had run a marathon and then replaced all my flesh with meat covered in fire ants. It was burning and stinging at the same time. My bones felt like lead and my lungs felt like they were being crushed.

I felt the pressure of hands against my body, the cool sticky feeling of latex gloves against my bare skin. There was a light in my eyes and the pressure and the pull of fingers against my eyelids, trying to make sure that my eyes were working.

Blinking, I managed to make out Doctor Alexander's face.

"Help me," I croaked.

"I'm trying," he replied gently, "I'm here now. I'm gonna help you."

I reached up to him, my weak, shaking fingers trying to find purchase in the white cotton of his lab coat. He wasn't wearing the hazmat suit.

41

His latex-covered fingers wrapped around mine and stopped the inhuman grabbing. I felt like I had lost control of everything.

"What happened?" he asked quietly.

I shook my head as I began to cough again. It didn't matter, really. I knew what was happening to me, even if there was no medical proof that demons existed. I was going to be eaten up by this curse the old woman had put on me.

"Oh my God." I heard Liam say as he pulled his hand away from mine. "What have you done to yourself?" he asked.

I wanted to answer, even though I knew it was a rhetorical question, but I couldn't find the strength to even do that. My mouth moved stupidly, like a grounded fish as I fought to breathe, and to answer his question. I couldn't speak, but the words bubbled in my mind. Finally, I began to pray. I will do anything, God, please, anything you ask, I will do. Please, God, let me go home and see my mom, just please make this pain stop. I will go to church every day, I'll convert to whatever religion you want, just please, heal me, give me a bit more time.

And for the second time that day, I fell into black, dreamless sleep.

DEPRESSION

I wasn't sure how long I was unconscious. It didn't matter anymore, really. I opened my eyes to find the same unforgiving white room around me. I tried to move my feet. I was lucky, there were no restraints this time. I felt so weak.

It took a moment but the memories all came flooding back. I was in the hospital. Something evil had happened to me. I was sick. I was dying. I had begged God to make it stop.

Everything still hurt, though, so God obviously hadn't heard my prayers.

I blinked and looked around. The filmy white bubble of the fumigation tent was gone. I wondered if that meant that I wasn't in quarantine anymore. I coughed and spluttered. My breathing sounded like I was underwater. Obviously the lung infection was back. It hurt. It felt like I was breathing in hot liquid. I wheezed inside the mask, trying to breathe against the coughing.

A loud beeping alarm began to ring as my heart rate spiked and my oxygen levels dropped. I was soon surrounded by hazmat suits and masks.

I tried to wave them away but they kept coming closer. Mercifully, someone turned off the alarm.

My bed began to move as the automated system pulled me into an upright sitting position. One of the masked nurses pulled the oxygen mask away from my face as the coughing began to subside She dabbed at my face with a cool cloth and wiped away the spittle that was clinging to my mouth.

"I'm thirsty," I whispered hoarsely.

"I'll bet," the reply came, though it wasn't from the hazmat suit in front of me.

I blinked stupidly as I watched the first paper suit move away from me and a new one take its place. It waved the other people who were buzzing around the room away and approached my bed.

"Doctor Alexander?" I asked quietly.

"Yes, it's me," he replied gently.

I looked up at him, only able to see his eyes from behind the mask he wore. If I hadn't been so weak, I would have blushed. I studied his eyes, the marginal wrinkles just starting around the corners, the dark circles underneath them. His skin was tanned, like he'd been enjoying the summer weather before he was called into work.

"I'm thirsty," I repeated weakly.

He nodded, his paper suit crinkling pleasantly, like wrapping paper on Christmas morning. I watched him pour a glass of water from the ever-present pitcher on the bedside table. He leaned over and offered it to me, holding the straw so that I didn't have to struggle with it.

"Slowly," he warned me. "You had an upset stomach earlier."

I narrowed my eyes in confusion and sipped slowly from the straw.

I pulled my dry lips away. "Thank you," I said with a frown. "I don't remember being sick," I added sheepishly.

The doctor turned away to place the cup back down but he wasn't quick enough to hide the shock from me.

"No, really," I said. "I don't know what you're talking about."

He was silent for a long moment. He fiddled with the cup and pitcher on the table and didn't say anything.

"What happened?" I asked, suddenly filled with dread. "I remember my parents coming to visit. Then I remember you taking about a million vials of blood, and another mouth swab and putting something new in my IV line. Then I woke up here."

The doctor took his protective goggles and the mask off his face and turned back to look at me. "You swear to me that you don't remember anything else?"

"I swear!" I said weakly. "I don't know what you're going on about, but that's all that I remember." I felt tears welling up in my eyes. "Please, tell me what's wrong," I begged.

Doctor Alexander sighed.

"Liam?" I asked, using his first name, trying to make him listen. "I'm scared," I said, the first of the tears falling freely down my face. "I'm sick, I know this. I know that it's worse than a flu. I know that you don't know what it is but you're trying to help. Please, I'm begging you, tell me what happened. Maybe I can help?"

"You got up," Liam said. "You pulled the oxygen mask off and you ripped the IV line out of your hand. You opened the tent that used to be here and you walked out. You got up, tore apart the room and threw up on the floor. When we..." He hesitated. "When I found you, you had taken a scalpel to the tent, tearing it apart and were on the floor sobbing and screaming as you pulled your hair out by the handful and gouged your fingernails into the wound on your hand."

I felt the heat leave my face and my stomach turned over.

"I... I what?" I stammered in disbelief.

45

"Your parents were called," he continued quickly. "I found you on the floor, screaming and sobbing and bleeding from wounds to your scalp. You had a fever that was off the charts. You fell asleep again in my arms, and we ended up sedating you and doing a quick surgery on the wound on your hand and on your scalp. You tore yourself up pretty badly."

"I didn't mean to," I said, sobbing. "Oh my God, I'm so sorry," I added. "I... I don't remember doing any of this."

"You were delirious when I found you," Doctor Alexander pressed. "You were babbling in your sleep, crying as you gouged your hand. You asked me to help you."

I nodded slowly.

"I sedated you, I got you back into bed," Liam explained. "We got your fever back down, barely. You were so scared, you... what possessed you to get up?"

I buried my face in my hands and sat there for a long moment, crying silently. "I didn't want to be in bed anymore. I didn't want to be sick anymore."

"I completely understand," he said, nodding sympathetically. "You've got a lot of fight in you, Zero. I like it. I know it's hard, but you gotta hang on. For me, mostly. I promise you that we're doing everything we can, and you just gotta let it work, okay?"

I nodded and would have blushed if I wasn't so anemic.

"How selfish am I? Using my ego to guilt you into healing. Next I'll bribe you with a date."

The sheer innocence of the joke make me laugh, which in turn sent me into another horrible coughing fit. This time it was violent and it managed to split my lower lip open, sending a fresh spray of blood onto the blanket on my lap.

"Shit," Liam cursed. He reached for a tissue and pressed it against my mouth.

"Sorry," I mumbled between coughs and through the tissue.

"Let me grab some gauze," he replied.

I watched him cross the room and grab a medical pad of gauze to press against my lip. I stared at him as he sat there, holding the gauze against my mouth with his blue-gloved hand. He was really handsome and he was honestly the only one who hadn't run away from me. He hadn't turned away from my blood-filled eyes. He was still here, talking to me even though I knew that I had lost so much weight that I looked emaciated. He still held my hand even though I had tried to gore it. He placed a gentle, comforting hand against my arm and when I looked I could see how thin and almost translucent my skin had become.

I felt tears filling my eyes again as he pulled the gauze gently away from my mouth.

"Let me look," he said gently. He prodded at my lower lip, examining the wound I'd made. He stood up and crossed the room again, dropping the gauze in the bio-hazardous waste container as he looked for something amongst the cabinets.

He came back in a moment with a tube of what I thought was something like Polysporin.

"It's a sealant," he explained as he dabbed a bit onto his blue vinyl finger. "Kind of like fake skin."

"Or super glue?" I asked as he gently spread a bit of the clear paste against my lips.

"Pretty much exactly like super glue," he agreed.

I smiled carefully to avoid splitting my dry lips any further. "Thank you."

"It's my job," he replied.

Way to kill the moment, doctor. I thought. "What else do you need to know?" I asked instead.

"Anything that you can think of that might be relevant," he said.

I shook my head. "I told you everything," I sighed. "I'm starting to think maybe this is some sort of curse? Maybe we need a witch doctor?"

Liam smiled for the first time in a long while. He patted my arm and it sent flutters up through my stomach.

I was breathing heavily, my heart rate had nearly doubled. My heart felt like it was going to kick through my chest and explode all over the bed sheets. The constant beeping of the heart monitor didn't even register in my mind.

We sat there in silence for a long, long moment.

"I'll be back in a little while," he promised, though his voice sounded far away.

A small smile touched my lips and I was asleep again before he had even left the room.

Good to his word, I woke up several hours later with my doctor sitting on the edge of my bed.

"What time is it?" I asked quietly, lifting my right hand to the oxygen mask, attempting to adjust it. My right hand had been bandaged over top of the wound I had made, and the nursing staff has subsequently tried to fix. I noticed then how bony and skeletal my hands had become, how my nails seemed abnormally long and claw-like. I stared at my hand, studying how grotesque they had become, the gauze hiding the horror I had done to myself. I noticed a strange, brownish spot on the gauze and wondered if I was still bleeding, or if it was old blood.

"It's just after midnight," Doctor Alexander told me gently. "I'm supposed to be going home now, but I thought I'd at least drop by to see you before I left."

"That's awfully kind of you," I mumbled, still distracted by the receding nail beds on my fingers.

Doctor Alexander cleared his throat, as if to remove something awkward from the conversation.

"Your parents stopped by to see you while you were unconscious. We decided it was best if we let you sleep through it this time though," he said after a moment.

"I appreciate that even more," I said with a small smile. My lip still felt numb where he'd super glued me back together. "I don't think that I can stand to deal with them much more." I sighed. "They take a lot out of me."

He nodded. "I could imagine. Do you want to give them some kind of message? Just in case there's something that prevents you from talking to them later?"

I shook my head.

"I'm not gonna die," I said defiantly, "and they know that I love them, so it's not a big deal. And I really don't have enough material possessions to warrant a will," I explained with a small shrug. "They can sort it out later."

"Fair enough," my doctor said.

"Hey?" I asked. "When I get out of here, when you cure me that is, would you like to maybe go get coffee with me?"

Liam wanted to smile, I could see it, but there was a bit more shock in his face. "I'm not technically supposed to fraternize with patients."

"I won't be a patient anymore," I countered, feeling bold as brass to have finally asked him out. "But you can still call me 'Zero' if you want," I added. "It's kind of a cute nickname."

He snorted a laugh. "It's not meant to be," he said quietly.

"I know," I replied sadly.

We sat there for a very long moment of awkward silence. He decided to break it first, probably to keep me talking before I fell back asleep, or into another coma.

"I have good news and bad news for you," he declared.

"Awesome," I mumbled, wincing suddenly as a new pain shot through me. "Can I request for you to up my dosage of morphine?" I asked before I allowed him to go on. "I can suddenly feel all sorts of horrific pain in my legs."

He shifted on the bed and lifted the blankets. It was then that I realized that I was no longer wearing my adorable cupcake pajama bottoms.

"What's it feel like?" he asked me, a very clinical tone of distance in his voice.

"Oh you know," I said wearily. "Kinda like my skin is being rent from my bones." I winced again as he poked me. "And a shooting pain up through my everything."

"Do you wanna know what's happening?" he asked me.

"Better to know than to have to guess," I replied, stifling a whimper.

"Your skin looks like it might have a flesh-eating disease attacking it. And there's a chance that you've got gangrene," he explained. "I'm gonna go sign back in and run a few tests overnight."

"Oh, don't do that," I told him, my voice sounded sleepy and drugged up to me. I only hoped that it didn't sound too pathetic to him. "You should go home, get some rest. I can sit here while my flesh is eaten by microbes overnight. I don't mind," I assured him without a trace of sarcasm, "and you can just amputate my toes tomorrow."

He laughed. Apparently I was still charming and amusing despite being drugged up on morphine and dying.

"No, I'll just go run the test," he assured me. "Sleep is for the weak." I wish I could have seen the smile dancing on his face. Even in these horrible conditions, and considering that we had an obvious connection, it was good to see that he could still smile in the face of my adversity. "Obviously the amount of antibiotics we're pumping into you isn't enough, there's a really good chance that I'll be operating on you tomorrow to remove the dead tissue."

"That's lovely," I replied, feeling my stomach rise and I almost wanted to throw up just thinking about it. "I still think that you could go home, sleep and just cut my legs off at the knees. I've always wanted to be half-robot. I'll even sign the waivers," I promised.

I felt him drape the sheets back over me. "As much as I appreciate your offer, Zero," he said. "I'll just make sure that we get this cleaned up."

"Do you always go above and beyond for all your patients?" I asked.

"Yes," he replied, "but I don't promise to take them all out to coffee after they're healthy."

I felt my heart skip a beat and the jump was noticed on the steady beeping of the heart monitor. If Doctor Alexander noticed, he didn't say anything, and for that I was thankful.

"I'll be back," he said. "I have to go sign in."

"What's this test involve?" I asked.

"A skin sample and a swab, why?"

"Take it now, the faster you can run the test, the better," I said. "Please, it hurts and I'm sure that it's been brought on by whatever this sickness is." I would have given him a very sad and puppy-like begging face if I'd had the strength, but as it was, I felt like I was about to cry, and throw up inside my oxygen mask.

There was only the slightest moment of hesitation as he weighed how much trouble he would get in if he did this thing.

"All right," he said finally. I heard some rustling noises as he looked for the medical equipment he needed.

I closed my eyes, preferring not to watch him take whatever samples he needed. I felt the blankets pulled back but I didn't feel him take his sample. I wasn't even aware that he had done anything until I felt his hand on my shoulder.

"Everything's done," he said.

I opened my eyes. "Did I fall asleep?" I asked.

He nodded. "Yeah, you did." He smiled. "But everything's ready. You'll be heading down to surgery soon. I'm going to have to remove the dead flesh from your legs and fix you that way," he explained. "It's unpleasant but it's the only way to make sure that we can stop the necrosis from spreading to the rest of your body."

I lifted my left hand, momentarily forgetting about the IV line taped firmly to it. I gave him a sincere thumbs up and nodded.

Liam smiled at me in return. "Okay. I'm gonna go now, I have to scrub in. Don't get sicker while I'm gone."

I gave him a weak smile. "No promises, Doc."

"You're really making me earn my pay this week," he teased me back. "Don't go anywhere. I'll see you in a few minutes."

SURGERY, SURGERY

Having my gurney pushed down the hallways to the operating room was a harrowing experience. I was forced into a mobile quarantine thing that made me look like I was in the glass coffin in the Disney version of Snow White.

I watched impassively as the lights rolled by overhead. I could see that I was being pushed by four hazmat suits and that we were taking the back hallways so that no one could see us.

I had heard them talking as they wheeled me around, apparently I was a big story. The precious Patient Zero was big news. The girl with the scary unidentifiable disease.

Joke was on them though. I was just going to completely recover from this virus once they got rid of whatever was attacking my flesh. The virus would disappear and it would all turn out to be a lung infection that was exacerbated by stress, altitude of flying and the generally unhealthy diet I'd had while travelling cross-country to look at schools. Not to mention the lack of sleep. I wasn't used to this sort of thing, and flying especially wasn't a thing I did often and combined with the flu I'd caught and the crazy amounts of drugs I'd been given it seemed to be no surprise that I had had a bad reaction to it all.

They'd probably blame tainted water for the bacteria infecting me in the first place. Mom would raise hell about the quality of our colleges and universities in this country, and do what she could to get me cheap tuition, because that's my mom. If they did blame bad water for this whole mess, then I could express the serious need for better options for the poor people suffering in Africa. Maybe I could write a paper about it and get into an Ivy League school or something.

I could just imagine it. I would get to state my case and raise more awareness for my passion in Africa, maybe even raise some money. The hospital would be famous for saving me, and the "Patient Zero School in the Holy Name of Saint Judas" in the remote, southern jungles Africa would be built and dedicated in my honour. Just the thought of something good coming out of my horrible suffering made me smile.

As long as someone was benefiting from this horror, I somehow seemed to be more relatively okay with the whole thing.

I watched the ugly green ceiling pass me, the lights zipping past. I felt like I was on the highway and the lights above me were streetlights guiding me. The babble of the nurses pushing me made no sense as I listened. There was a lot of technical stuff that I didn't understand, mixed with a bit of apprehension coming through in their conversation.

I didn't blame them. I wouldn't want to be in charge of carting around the girl with the disease that could potentially infect everyone who came into contact with her either.

Finally, we slowed and there was a momentary jolt as the bottom of the stretcher bumped into the swinging doors that led to the operating room. I'd never seen the inside of one before, and I was amazed at how big it actually was.

The walls were all grey. Or at least, they looked grey in the dim light. The walls were tall and ominous, the room seemed to be slightly domed above us. There was a space in the middle of the room where I assumed the operating table was, and above this, there were what looked like a few dozen different kinds of lights. It was definitely not very inviting in here and I was immediately uncomfortable to be there. It felt about as inviting as a mortuary and as sterile as my quarantine room. I couldn't see much else about the room, which was probably for the better. I didn't even see any familiar monitors or machinery. It was good, I decided. I didn't want to see anything that was going to poke, prod or otherwise monitor me while I was unconscious.

An interesting thought flitted through my head. I wondered if it was going to be like on the television shows, where major operations were observed from the balcony observation room. Maybe the Dean was going to watch as my doctor tried to save my life. Or maybe there would be some students up there watching in mute fascination and horror as they removed thin pieces of my flesh to get rid of the necrosis that was otherwise devouring me alive.

Maybe, I thought, maybe one of those fresh-faced youngsters would see me down on the table and see what was happening. Maybe he would have a copy of my chart and have read my case. I was positive that I would be a case study for years, regardless of the outcome of it all. Maybe this kid who was working his way up through the doctor ranks and trying to make a name for himself in the world of medicine, would see me and start pounding on the glass that separated the actual operation room from the observatory.

This young upstart from a low-income family and a bad neighbourhood would have a sudden flash of insight. He would start pounding on the glass and shout for everyone to hear him. "Wait!" he would say, telling at the top of his lungs. "Don't just take off the dead flesh!" he'll exclaim. "There is an underlying cause above and beyond! It's not just

flesh-eating disease! It's not even necrosis! You have to..."
And he would finish his sentence with a boatload of medical
gibberish that I couldn't possibly make up even on a good
day. The surgery would stop part way through.

My doctor would order someone to scrub him in and this
young kid would come into the operating room and explain
to my handsome and intelligent Liam that there was another
thing that they hadn't tested for that was presenting as flesh-
eating disease and that they had to do something completely
different if they had any hope in hell of saving me.

Then Liam would stop and stare at this kid. This intern of
all things. And he would consider his words. And then Liam
would stare at my unconscious, dying form lying motionless
and horrifying in my degeneration. He would make a choice.

"Do what the kid says," he would instruct his nurses.
"But," he would add to this upstart young intern, "if you're
wrong, and she dies on this table, you will have to answer for
that." He would stare the kid down. "Can you deal with the
trauma of losing her?"

They would stare at each other for a long, tense moment.
And the kid would nod.

"Good!" Liam would yell. "Prep her for this new
operation! Let's save Zero!"

The gurney stopped under the brightest lights I had ever
had the displeasure of being exposed to. I closed my eyes
against them as my Snow White coffin of quarantine was
removed from around me. The hazmat suits each took a
moment to whisper good luck to me and then they were
gone.

A new figure towered over me.

"Hey Zero." It was Liam. "Can you hear me?" he asked.

I nodded.

"Good," he replied gently. "Now listen very carefully. Do
you understand what is about to happen to you?"

56

You are going to cut pieces of my body off in thin layers until you are sure that you have removed all of the dead and decaying flesh from me. If it is running too deep or too extensive, you will have to consider amputation.

I wish I could have spoken, but I merely nodded again.

"Your parents have been informed of what's going to happen to you," he told me. "They have signed all the paperwork on your behalf as you aren't lucid enough to speak for yourself."

I nodded. That much was apparent even to me.

"If we can't remove the necrosis from you in a timely manner, or if there is too much to remove safely, we will consider amputation. Your parents have agreed to this should it become necessary."

I felt tears welling up in my eyes. I had never cried so much in my life as I had since I'd been taken to the hospital. I really didn't like the thought of losing a limb because I'd started to rot while I was alive, but I nodded again.

"All right, Zero," Liam said more gently and with a more intimate tone than I think even he had intended. "We're gonna put you under now. You'll be asleep while we do this, and you'll wake up back in the quarantine room, hopefully feeling much better."

"Thank you..." I mumbled as the anesthetic began to pump into my veins.

I was unconscious before I could hear his reply.

When I woke up, I was in the quarantine room, just as Doctor Alexander had promised. I felt strange, lightweight, like part of me was missing. I sat very still and very quiet, still too weak to actually sit up. I tried to move my toes but even that felt like too much work.

A moment of panic washed over me.

Had they actually cut off my legs? Had the disease eaten me that far that they had to take me apart? I didn't really want to be a cyborg, that had been a joke.

My breathing became erratic and I knew that it was bad for me but I couldn't help it. I huffed deeply, my breaths bubbling with the liquid that filled my lungs and rattled in my chest. My heart rate sped up until the beeping of the monitor became a wail.

I didn't care if I was about to go into shock or have a heart attack, I needed to know if I was intact and I was too weak to find out for myself.

"Help!" I mumbled as my chest began to tighten up.

Another alarm went off, and I felt my entire body flush with heat. Something bad was happening inside me and there was no on around to tell me what it was. And on top of it all, I was probably missing at least one leg!

My chest heaved and I struggled against the bed, trying to sit up, trying to get someone's attention. The beeping and the waling alarms made my head feel like it was about to burst open and spill my brains all over the floor.

I almost hoped that it would, just so that I could be done with this suffering.

I felt my muscles begin to tighten up like my chest. I felt a sheer sweat break out on my forehead. My breathing was a thin whisper as I struggled. I was hot and cold and unable to breathe.

Suddenly, masked faces appeared at my bedside.

"She's seizing!" someone shouted.

I felt the oxygen mask pull free from my face as my mouth began to fill with foamy saliva. I felt the tremors begin to shake my body as my temperature climbed even higher. I gasped and choked for breath as the tremors grew into full out spasms and my body leaped against the flat bed. I could suddenly feel my legs as they shook and my panic was quelled.

Unfortunately, the seizure wasn't as easily stopped. I felt my core tighten and spasm and the whole bed shook as the masks around me hovered and tried to hold me steady.

"She's bleeding!" someone shouted.

"That's not normal..." someone else added.

I didn't know at the time, but my blood was congealing in my veins. It was coming out blackish brown and was thickening inside me.

"Sedate her!" I heard my doctor's voice call out. "She's bleeding from her eyes and nose? Sedate her! We have to operate again."

I wanted to scream, it all hurt so bad, and the last thing I felt was the needle gouge my arm where they filled me with sedatives. I was unconscious again.

I woke up shaking with cold. I hoped that my fever had finally broken and that I was cold from lack of blankets. It was wishful thinking. There were faces fluttering around me, all doing some important task or another. Apparently, something had happened while I was unconscious.

"Hey?" I mumbled. The oxygen mask was firmly against my face.

"She's awake, Doctor," one of the nurses said flatly.

A mask floated in front of my face. I recognized the eyes.

"Doctor?" I whispered.

"You're getting worse," he said quietly. "One of your eyes has filmed over like a cataract. The wounds on your scalp and on your hand have gone septic, so we're pumping you full of steroids and penicillin," he explained. "Don't panic. We're doing everything we can to fix you."

"So cold..." I murmured.

"I know sweetie," my doctor said. "You have a fever. We're trying to bring the temperature down to a reasonable level. If your temperature stays this high, you're gonna have a seizure again."

I shook my head, then I realized that I was lying flat on my back. I swallowed in fear.

"What are you going to do to me?" I asked, though I only got out half the sentence before my words became garbled.

"We're bringing your temperature down first," Liam told me, "then we're going to try scrubbing your veins."

"What?" I asked, I was too weak and tired to cry.

"We're gonna give you a full blood transfusion."

If I had been more lucid, I would have argued, but the words made no sense to me. The beeping and buzzing of the room drowned out all logical words. I felt myself falling back asleep, whether it was because of my sickness or because of the anesthetic, I couldn't say. I just knew that I was sick, scared and the concept of a radical treatment scared me beyond words.

"Help..." I mumbled.

"I am," Liam assured me. "Go to sleep. We'll talk when you wake up."

SWEET DREAMS

I stood in front of the mirror, making sure that my clothing looked all right.

I had picked out a floral patterned dress to wear and a pair of cute, but sensible shoes. My hair was thin and ratty, still not entirely healed from where I had pulled it out, but a wide brimmed sun hat covered it up and generally completed the outfit.

I stared at myself in the mirror. Despite the food I'd been eating since I'd gotten out of the hospital, I was still rail thin, but I had begun to fill out a little more. I was eating solid foods again, at least.

I looked at the angry scar on my right hand and shuddered. The ordeal in the hospital was still fresh in my mind. I was still shaken by the whole thing. Part of me was amazed that I had come through it. I smiled to myself.

With a sigh I took one last look at myself in the mirror. I wasn't pretty. I was far from pretty. I had scars on my legs from where they had removed the necrosis. I had a scar on my hand from my own insanity. My hair was thin and stringy and there were still scars on my scalp where I might never get hair back. One of my eyes was still milky white with cataracts, and there was an indent in my lower lip where it had broken, but I was on the mend, more or less.

It was a great day to be alive. The sun was out, the birds were singing and I was about to go on my promised coffee date with Doctor Liam Alexander.

I smiled to myself, carefully as I was still wary of the split in my lip. I walked slowly down the stairs from my bedroom. I was sore and would be for a while. I'd been through hell and back and the scars and aches of my trials were going to be sticking around for a while.

My parents were thrilled to have me back. They had thrown a party when I'd been strong enough.

It was a strange feeling, to be home, to be whole. It was good, mostly.

I felt like there was a huge part of me that I had left behind in the sterile rooms of the hospital. It felt like I had walked away from a car crash and had lost a finger in the wreckage. I might have been lucky enough to walk out of the hospital mostly intact, but part of my soul just wouldn't come back.

My parents were in the kitchen, laughing and I said my goodbyes.

Mom smiled and wished me luck.

Dad told me to be back by sunset.

I didn't make any promises.

Liam was waiting outside for me when I opened the door.

"You look beautiful," he said quietly.

"Thank you," I said, blushing.

I smiled and looked him over. He was wearing a pair of jeans and a plain shirt that was the same colour as his scrubs. His hair was slicked back and his eyes weren't as tired as I'd seen them in the hospital.

"Nice shirt," I said sarcastically.

He looked down at his shirt. "What's wrong with it?" he asked as I stepped out of my house and closed the door.

"Well, for starters, it's hospital scrub green," I replied easily, entwining my fingers with his. "Let's go to the cafe," I said, changing the subject before he could object to my observations about his taste in clothes.

He smiled brightly. "I thought we could walk?" he asked me.

"You have a car right there," I pointed out, making a vague motion to his nondescript car parked in front of my house.

"As your doctor, I think it would be more beneficial to your healing body, as well as our budding relationship, if you walked the five blocks to the chain coffee joint where we shall be enjoying our first cup of coffee as potential partners," he replied using his best doctor-like voice on me.

I laughed. "All right," I agreed. "As long as it's supervised and monitored by my doctor."

"I will take only clinically detached pleasure in watching you walk because it means you're healing nicely," he promised.

We walked quietly to the cafe, hand in hand. It was a little hard to breathe. I obviously wasn't entirely healed, but I didn't fall over and he didn't complain about how slow and unsteady I was.

He pulled the chair out from the outdoor table for me and I sat down primly, smoothing my skirt against my legs.

"What would my lady friend like to drink?" Liam asked me.

"Something cold and tasting of coffee," I replied.

Liam smiled and bowed. "I can do that," he informed me.

I couldn't help but stare as he walked away. The jeans were definitely an improvement over the scrubs and the paper hazmat suit that I had grown so accustomed to seeing him in. I smiled to myself and turned my face up towards the sky, taking in the first real sunshine I had seen since I had been admitted to the hospital.

I sighed.

I wouldn't have had coffee if I hadn't pulled through.

The thought was a sudden, devastating jolt and it twisted my stomach into knots. I had made it through, right? I was sitting here, at the cafe, with my doctor, on a date. I was out of the hospital, I was home. Wasn't I?

I stared at the table, pressing my hands against it.

"This is real!" I said to myself. "This is where I am now. I have made it beyond the reach of that damned disease! I am alive."

I clenched my hands and pounded them against the table, tears welling up in my eyes. My heart was breaking and I was hyperventilating. I didn't even care who saw me crying, I was scared and needed reassurance.

I heard a jingling noise as Liam was suddenly by my side.

"Are you crying?" he asked me.

"Yes," I replied earnestly.

"Why are you crying?"

"Because I'm dying," I said slowly. "I'm still dying, and there's nothing you can do to save me."

Liam smiled briefly but his smile didn't linger. It began to fade until his face was a blank mask, devoid of all emotion.

"Liam?" I asked quietly, unsure of what was happening. "Liam?"

"I've done all I can," he said in a perfect monotone. "I can't help you anymore. You're on your own. Either you fight it and get through it, or you succumb."

I let out a small shriek of horror.

Everything around me grew suddenly very quiet. I was afraid that I was hallucinating, that I was relapsing and that I was about to have a seizure. I felt my heart rate spike and my skin started to get very warm.

I stared at Liam. He stared back, but he wasn't Liam anymore. His eyes were dead, his hair was falling out, his teeth rotten and black. He reached for me, the smell of death and the grave coming off of him in waves. I tried not to throw up. I wanted to scream. I stumbled as I fought to get up from the table. I could feel the tears welling up in my eyes as what used to be Liam let out an inhuman groan. His groan was accompanied by another, and another until all of the patrons at the cafe were lumbering, slowly, dead and rotting.

"I'm sorry," I begged, tripping over my own weak legs, and unable to get away as I slumped back down into my seat. I was too weak to do anything but apologize. "I'm so sorry..."

My heart hammered in my chest, I huffed, my breathing was getting erratic as fear gripped me tight. I heard a beeping and a ringing in my ears, so close to the sounds of the hospital. I gripped my chest, afraid that I was going to pass out and have a seizure. My right hand gripped the table so hard that the stitches that I thought had healed ripped out and blackish brown blood oozed out of the wound and on to the table. I let out a sob and my lip split open again, adding to the dripping, bloody mess on the table and soaking into my dress.

The beeping got louder.

My eyes snapped open and I was in my hospital bed, sobbing as my body writhed in an uncontrollable spasm against the mattress and nurses tried to hold me steady.

I gasped for breath, trying to tell them that I was all right; there was nothing to worry about.

I had been dreaming.

ACCEPTANCE

The full blood transfusion nearly killed me.

I woke up five days later. Apparently, they kept me in a drug-induced coma for almost a week after the surgery failed to make me better. The bitter part of me inside wanted to laugh at their stupidity. They'd just wasted eight pints of blood trying to fix me.

I just hoped that they wouldn't try organ transplants next.

The hopeful part said that maybe now I would have a better chance to live. They'd cleaned out my blood, technically, and so maybe the disease would have to work hard to get a new hold on me. I tried to hold on to that thought for as long as possible but it was fleeting at best. My mind was pretty much made up. I was ready to accept the fact that they couldn't cure me without knowing what it was. Part of me was ready to make peace with the fact that there was no hope for me and that I was dying.

I was lying flat on my back again. I smacked my lips together. My mouth was so dry. It didn't matter though, I couldn't feel anything and I knew that I was too weak to call out for help. I couldn't even lift my arm to move the plastic mask that felt like it was suffocating me.

I hated the white walls in here. They were so bland and horrifying. It wasn't a welcoming place that I was in. This white room was my death sentence. I laughed internally, too weak to laugh aloud. My mom had been right. I was going to die in the quarantine room.

I sighed and let my head drop to one side, trying to get a better view of what was happening around me. It was so quiet. Even the beeping of the friendly heart monitor seemed quieter today, like it was far away.

I managed to catch a glimpse of my reflection in one of the machines nearby and I almost screamed. I looked skeletal. My face had lost all of the weight in it. My flesh was just hanging on to my skull. Where I'd once had full cheeks and a touch of a baby-faced look about me there was nothing but loose flesh and bone. My eyes were sunken, hollow and dead inside the sockets. Dark circles rimmed my eyes and I noticed that one was milky white, just as Liam had said before, and the other was still red with broken blood vessels. I wondered how that was possible if they'd taken out all my blood, but assumed that I would never get an answer.

I sniffled underneath the oxygen mask and closed my eyes. I was too weak to pull my head back to a neutral position. I wanted to cry, but even that seemed like too much work, so I laid there in the silence, listening to the familiar beeping of the heart monitor and wondered if it was so quiet because my heart is so weak.

My mind began to wander, recalling memories and goals, things that I was before I got sick. I can see my family in my mind's eye. They are perfect, smiling and waving. There are kids running around on the neighbour's lawn, my mom is perfectly made up as usual and my dad has a five o'clock shadow.

I think about my friends and I pray that I haven't infected them. I hope that they aren't sick from when I came home and they were sitting in my house. I hope that the Smiths aren't sitting next to another bed where their daughter lays sick and dying like me. I couldn't live with it if it was true. I hope that they would remember me fondly from it, and not from the skeletal monstrosity that I had become.

A sudden rustle in the room alerted me to the fact that I wasn't alone. I opened my eyes momentarily to see a white hazmat suit bustling about doing something that I didn't really want to know about. I sighed and closed my eyes again, wondering when I would get to see Liam. He really was handsome. He should have been an actor or something. He could have played a doctor on TV instead. The thought brought a little smile to my face.

I kind of wished then for that miracle to happen. I really did want to go and get a coffee with him after this was all said and done. He'd taken extra care of me, I couldn't help but notice him. And now that I was in quarantine, I assumed he'd been in his own quarantine. They couldn't risk having him spread the infection.

I wondered how many people they had to quarantine because of me. I couldn't bear it if there were a platoon of nurses who were shoved into a white room having constant tests run on them because of me. I didn't think that they deserved that. Not even the redheaded one who had stabbed me mercilessly with the needle on the first day I had been in the hospital.

No one deserved this sickness. I wouldn't wish this on anyone. I just hoped that when I was gone, they could use my organs to find a cure for this.

As soon as I had that thought, I realized, that I was resigned to my fate. The sudden dawning of this realization struck me like a hammer blow. I was dying. I'd been aware of it for a long time, but I hadn't really accepted it until now.

They had stopped calling me by name, instead referring to me as 'the subject'. Or 'the patient'. Even my doctor, Liam, hadn't called me by name for a while. He had started calling me 'Zero' and I thought it was cute. I never considered that he was doing it to distance himself from me. I wonder how long he'd been aware that I wasn't going to make it.

The pain of the thought that he had been aware that I was dying hurt worse than the fire in my lungs or the peeling, burning sensation of my skin. I wondered if he'd promised me a coffee date because he knew that I wasn't going to make it.

I hoped that he had told my parents.

Another rustle, closer this time pulled me from my thoughts again. I heard a quiet jingle, too.

A bell? Or keys, maybe?

I forced my eyes open, staring up at the hazmat suit standing above me.

"Liam?" I tried to whisper. My mouth wouldn't make the noise though. It came out as a choked wheeze. I couldn't even apologize.

The suit leaned forward, blue-gloved hands gently moved my head back to the neutral position.

"Hey, Zero," Liam said.

If I had had the strength, I would have argued that Zero wasn't my name and he should be more polite than to call me by my case number, even though I had loved the nickname. I longed for human contact, something to tell me that yes, I was still alive, even if I was barely hanging on. I stared at him through my milky, ruined eyes, wishing I could talk to him, tell him anything, have him tell me something that wasn't medical garbage.

"I don't know if you can hear me anymore, but I just wanted you to know that your parents are coming to see you. They'll be here in about an hour, so don't go anywhere, all right?" he continued.

"Yes!" I said.

All he heard was a gurgle.

"I can't understand what you're trying to tell me," Doctor Alexander said with a sigh. "You haven't been able to speak for a while," he explained. "Not since before the blood transfusion. I'm so sorry."

I blinked slowly, forcing my head to nod. I wanted to tell him that it was all right, that I wasn't angry. I knew he had done everything that he could for me. That there was nothing anyone could do. I wasn't even sure if I was awake or if this was a horrible dream. Maybe I was imagining all of this. Maybe I was still in a drug-induced coma from the operation and they had me under observation, waiting to see if I got stronger.

Maybe this was the dream? Maybe this was all a nightmare and I was really at home, in my bed. Maybe I had already had my coffee date with Liam and we'd made plans to go out to a movie, or to dinner. This had to be a bad dream, things were too bad for this to be real, right? I was desperate with hope. Hope that this was all a nightmare and that I would wake up soon enough.

"So, I said we would talk," he said slowly. "So I'm gonna talk to you, even if you're too far gone to hear me anymore." He sighed, and it sounded like his heart was breaking. "I wanted you to know that I never thought that you would end up like this," he began slowly. "I think you're a brilliant, smart, kind, beautiful young lady and I was really looking forward to taking you up on that offer for coffee." He sighed sadly. "I tried everything that I could to heal you. I thought that the blood transfusion might have bought us some extra time to fix you. I thought that, as radical as it was, maybe if we could get the infected blood out of your system and replace it with clean blood, maybe it would have flushed out the sickness.

"I was wrong. Or maybe I didn't think to do it fast enough," he continued, still apologizing. "At any rate, I feel like my mistakes have cost you your life," he told me gently. "I just wanted you to know that I'm sorry, that I tried and that I'm blaming myself for this."

I wanted to reach out for him just then, to tell him that I forgave him and to absolve him from his guilt. But I was too weak to do anything but listen.

"I hate to see you here like this," he said. "I want you to know that we got the necrosis before we had to amputate and that if you manage to pull through this you'll heal nicely." He smiled for me then and I could see the tears glistening in his eyes. He was too macho to cry, though, and I knew that he had to try to maintain a professional attitude, but the tears let me know that he was sincere.

"I really had hoped that I would... No, I wanted you to come through this," he told me. "And I know that there's still hope... There's always hope." He paused for a moment, wiping his eyes. "And I don't know how else to give you hope."

I would have given anything to have been able to reach out for him. I wanted to talk to him, to reassure him.

Liam, Liam, I thought. I couldn't do much more than groan. *You've done more for me than I could have thought Please don't worry. Please, it's okay.*

The pain in his eyes was more than I could bear. I closed my eyes. He was so gentle, so kind. He broke all sorts of protocol to make sure that no one else got infected, and to make sure that I wasn't alone. He cared too much and now there was nothing he could do but watch me suffer. I didn't deserve him, and he didn't deserve to lose me like this.

"I hope that I chased out your demons," he said quietly.

He stood up from his spot on the edge of my bed. He was the only one who sat with me in here. Not even my parents had dared to touch me, let alone come near me like that. Everyone was too afraid of the girl in quarantine.

Another rustle joined the first one and my doctor was suddenly involved in a conversation with another hazmat suit. That was all right, he'd said hello. Maybe, just maybe, I would get my miracle.

I closed my eyes and waited.

The next thing I remembered was the sound of a woman sobbing. I took a deep breath, sucking in the oxygen that streamed steadily from the mask and I opened my eyes.

"Oh! She's awake!" a gentle male voice said.

I blinked slowly and turned my head. Two masks, two sets of eyes and two more of the horrible hazmat suits that haunted my waking hours. One set of eyes was red-rimmed and had mascara running under the mask.

It was my parents, I knew it.

"Mom," I said, "Dad."

"Why does she sound like that?" Mom asked. "Why is she making that horrible noise?"

Dad placed his arm around my mom. I just watched them, so stricken with grief, so nonsensical in the scary white suits that made them faceless entities.

I wanted to tell them to pray for a miracle, but I couldn't. I couldn't even lift my hand, let alone move my fingers. I sighed to myself and closed my eyes. I didn't want to see them any longer than I had to.

Mom's sobbing permeated my thoughts, and I felt a hand against my arm, gentle as though I was fragile. I suppose I was fragile, now. I never thought that I would end up here, in a hospital bed, not at age eighteen.

I wanted to do something to tell everyone that I was all right. I wanted them to know how much I appreciated everything that they had all done for me. I would have given anything for a few minutes to speak coherently with everyone, even my parents. I would tell them I loved them, and I would apologize for scaring them so badly. I would have taken all the blame, all the guilt that I imagined that my parents must have been feeling for me right then and there. I would have assured them that it was all right.

I wanted to talk to my doctor. I wanted to tell Liam how I really felt. I wanted to admit my feelings, to tell him that I wanted nothing more than to get to know him better outside of the hospital. And to yell at him for keeping his distance.

I wanted to laugh at stupid jokes. I wanted to hug my best friend. I wanted... I wanted to go outside. I wanted to go home.

There was nothing I could do, though. Nothing the doctors could do. Their "Patient Zero" would die soon enough.

DEATHBED

I used to have a name. I was born and raised by my parents. They loved me, They raised me to do what's right, whenever I could, and to never back down on my morals. I was normal. I lived in a cookie-cutter, suburban house. I played with toys and watched too much television. I loved to read books, and I rode a bike with pink ribbons on the handlebars when I was younger.

My parents loved me. They gave me a name.

Now though, the doctors and nurses who buzz around me day in and day out have stopped calling me by name. They haven't used my name for a long time. They refer to me as "The Patient" or "Our Subject" or worse, by "Jane Doe." Sometimes, they call me "Zero," and that's the only one that seems remotely like a nickname. I liked it, at first, but now I realize that they are trying to distance themselves from me. I know they're not doing it maliciously, but they are trying to dehumanize me, trying to make me into a case study, a number to scrutinized instead of a living, breathing person.

I know it must be hard for them to see me like this, and to have seen me deteriorate every day. I watch them through cloudy eyes as they draw vial after vial of my abnormal blood. I can see their eyes over the masks they wear to avoid contamination. They all say the same thing with their looks of mixed fear and apology, "Sorry this is happening."

I can't imagine how hard it must be for them, to watch me deteriorate in front of them and to not be able to do a damn thing about it. Even their fancy degrees and medical equipment can't save me, it seems. I don't blame them, they're just people, too, after all.

I stopped wondering if they'll be able to keep me alive long enough to fix me.

My life has become so little, now. I am hooked up to machines that monitor my heart. I am hooked up to machines that help me breathe. There are more tubes running from my arms than I have fingers, and the liquids inside the tubes are every colour of the rainbow. I don't know what they are, but I assume that they're supposed to be helping keep me alive. I've been reduced to a number and a series of machines, more robotic than human, I guess.

So here I am. Lying nameless in the hospital.

I've lost count of how long I have been in here. It seems like forever, but it's probably less than that. I feel like all the memories of sunshine and grass and fresh air are not memories at all. Only dreams, and things that my subconscious made up to help me cope with what's happening to me.

I can see the nurses flinch when I cough. It sounds horrible, even to me. I can feel my muscles protest as my core tightens up and I shake in the bed. My lungs feel like they're full of liquid and fire and I can't breathe. I wheeze, trying to get the oxygen that I need to keep fighting, but it's getting harder. The mask is slipped over my face and I can barely feel my lungs taking in the precious gas. The coughing subsides and one of the nurses moves my mask just enough to dab the spittle off of my face. I can see that it's an unhealthy colour. Not quite brown, but certainly not entirely green anymore either. The tissue is put in a biohazard bag and put in the proper receptacle.

I can smell the rubber of the gloves, and the sweat of the doctors and nurses. I am constantly surrounded by these hovering faces, these masks and eyes. They are just eyes to me now. I don't know if these are the same people who helped me when I first came in. I was sick; they assumed it was nothing, a bug or virus I'd picked up from my cross-country travels. I have been in quarantine now, since my condition got worse. I wonder what happened to the doctors and nurses who initially treated me. Are they as sick as I am? Did I infect the really cute orderly who helped me into the hospital when I puked on his shoes? Did that awful nurse who stuck me too many times with the needle get infected by my blood? Or is this just something trapped inside my body alone? I hope I haven't infected anyone else. I couldn't live with myself if there was another person suffering this way because of me.

Days have passed without time, without reason. There's no routine to my days. I'm sick. I'm awake. I'm asleep. There are tubes. There are faces. I see the faces hovering above me and I wonder when they sleep, do they take turns? Do they sleep when I sleep? Are these the same people as before? I don't know. The faces clean my face with a cool cloth to try and fight off the fever that seems to have become a constant for me. The tubes are changed, the liquids drip, the machines beep and drone. I am sick again, my body shakes as I retch and heave, or convulse, sometimes both. My vomit is black. I see my skin, pale and ashen. I feel like I am a corpse already, but I just refuse to give up. My hair is stringy and thin, almost gone. My fingernails stopped growing and my skin is paper-thin. I am grotesque, but they still try to save me. I haven't eaten in God knows how long, but the vitamins in the IV lines keep me alive. I must look skeletal to them.

I fear sleep. I never know when it's going to come, or if I'm going to wake up again. I fall asleep and wake up and there are more faces. Are they the same faces? I don't know. They give me more drugs to make me sleep, like it will be better for me if I just sleep. They ask me if I want to be put into a drug-induced coma. It will help with the pain, they say. I won't feel anything anymore, they assure me. They'll keeps irking to cure me. I keep refusing. I'm over eighteen, they don't have to ask my parents. I'm positive that they have asked my parents, though. I'm in no position to make my own decisions.

Now that I think about it, I don't remember when the last time that I saw my parents was. I don't know if they've been back to see me. All the faces look the same behind the masks. I know I saw them before, I remember my mother crying. Everything is so fuzzy and muddled, was that before the surgery? Did they come see me after they blood transfusion? I wonder where they are. Are they here, watching me, waiting for me to get better? Praying that the next insane treatment that the doctors think up will be the one that resets my system and cures me?

I cough again. I swear that every time I cough I am going to tear my lungs out, or cough up my heart. It's painful to cough, and the phlegm and spittle that comes out of my mouth worries me worse than the black vomit or the thick brown blood that they've been removing from my veins.

Everything hurts. I've never felt so much pain in my entire life. My skin feels like it is peeling away from my flesh and my flesh feels like it is peeling away from my bones. My bones feel like my skeleton is trying to claw its way out from its place inside of me. My lungs are full of fire, breathing is difficult. My stomach feels like it has been liquefied and has been replaced by acid. My lips are cracked and bleeding and my tongue feels three sizes too big for my mouth. My fingers are skeletal claws, my nails have chipped and withdrawn. I can see my knuckles protruding from through my paper-thin skin. I haven't seen my legs in weeks. I'm positive that I can't move them, and that I've grown too weak now to even wiggle my toes.

I let my head flop lazily to the side and I can see my arm. I am so thin, it's startling. The needles in my arm are raised lumps under my skin. I can see the darker shadow they cast under my pallid flesh. I don't think that I can see my veins anymore, and I vaguely wonder if they've collapsed.

I can hear my breath rattling, it sounds like there's something loose in my chest, in my lungs. The fire is always there, always constant. Even the morphine that the doctors are constantly pumping into me can't dull the pain anymore.

I shiver suddenly. A chill passes over me, and I feel the shakes set in and stay. I'm so cold, but so hot. I can feel the perspiration break out against my body, cold and clammy. The shivers begin to intensify and I can see my arm shuddering against the bed. If I had any strength left I would have drawn up the blankets, or curled in upon myself. But there was nothing left in me. I'd been in a state of steady decline, my health was getting worse and there was nothing they could do could help me.

I begin to cough, my body arching against the bed as my slight frame shakes with the wheezing, horrible coughs that have plagued me from the beginning. I feel my lips split open wider and I can feel the warmness of the thick black blood that oozes from the open wound dribble down my chin and pool inside the oxygen mask that has become a part of my face.

The beeping machines begin to scream as my heart rate spikes. My temperature is rising, I feel like I am on fire. The masked faces monitoring me float around me in a tizzy. I can't understand what they are saying, but they're worried. Machines continue to scream and beep at them as they scramble to figure out what's wrong. I hear the word 'stabilize' and 'heart attack'. It's not a heart attack, I think, wishing that I could tell the doctors and nurses what's going on in my mind. I'm panicking.

The oxygen mask is pulled away from my face and the blood pooling inside spills down my chin, black and glistening. My coughing somehow manages to get worse. I reach for the mask that they take away from me. I can't breathe, help me.

It's the eyes again. Nothing but masks and eyes. The eyes all display their sympathies, they all say how sorry they are that this has happened to me. They're all saddened by the steady decline in my health. And yet they can't do a damn thing but apologize.

New drugs are put in the various tubes and I can feel the new solutions dripping into my hypersensitive veins. I can see through the milky haze that has covered my once-blue eyes that they're preparing the defibrillator. They don't expect me to come out of this one, and yet they'll do anything to keep me alive for just a bit longer.

The coughing subsides for a moment of reprieve and my heart rate slows down a bit. I can see the mask holding the defibrillator lower the paddles slowly.

I gasp, a wheezy noise that sounds far weaker that it had even moments before.

I'm perfectly aware that I'm not long for this world. I am resigned to that fact. I just hope that I didn't infect anyone else. I would never forgive myself if I had.

No, I tell myself, *let's not sugar coat it, Zero. You're dying. You've put up the good fight, kid. But now it's time to go. You've been reduced to this aching, burning, fevered shell of your once glorious self. Don't hide it from yourself. You're not you anymore. You're Zero.*

I close my eyes and I can feel hot tears welling up behind my eyelids. Part of me laughs at that. I wasn't aware that I had any tears left in me. I know that I wasn't always this way. I know that I used to live a normal life, a good life. At least, I tried to be good. I have a moment to look back on my life, to reflect. I know what I have done, and who I helped in my short time on this planet. Maybe I could look back just a bit longer. Maybe that will give me the strength to keep fighting. I feel the pull of my thoughts, struggling to gain traction as I watch the drugs drip from their lines and into my body. My mind wanders as the narcotics start to kick in again. I can't feel anything anymore. The pain is gone, I am weightless, floating through memory and passing in and out of consciousness. I snap awake again despite the drugs, despite the sleep that the doctors want to force on me. I look around the room and I know I can't. I let myself think about my family, my friends. I think about growing up, about school. I think about my illness, and about all the good I wanted to do in this world. Finally, I think about all the coffee dates that I wanted to have with Liam. About the places I'd never get to go, about the things that I wanted to do, but can't. I have nothing left in me, and I can't fight it.

I suddenly nod lazily, gasping for breath as my fever starts to climb higher and sets off a new buzzing alarm.

"Tell my parents goodbye," I try to speak. It doesn't work, my throat is parched, my vocal chords have torn themselves apart from all the coughing. I gnash my teeth as my broken lips try to form the words.

Another cough wracks my body and I shake my head.

I gnash my teeth again, unintentionally. The fever reaches its apex and the masks of the doctors around me begin to move again. Tears roll down my cheeks and I swear to you, they evaporated before they could totally fall. The fever was burning its way through me. My veins were on fire. My skin was melting under the heat of the fever. I could feel it in my brain, boiling me alive. I wanted to apologize, to say my goodbyes, and to thank the doctors for trying but there is nothing of me left.

I closed my eyes, my time had come at last.

I let out a peaceful sigh, I have made my peace and I'm ready to go.

They weren't ready for me to seize. My body tenses up and begins to shake. My lungs collapse within my chest. My heart rate spikes again, setting off another alarm. The rapid beating of my heart hammers against the inside of my chest. I wince internally as my heart feels like it's about to explode, and then it stops.

"She's crashing!" I hear one of the masks exclaim.

But I'm already gone before the first jolt from the defibrillator shocks my chest.

EPILOGUE

The wheels of the gurney squeaked as he rolled it down the cold, stark, white hallway. The florescent lights flickered ominously. It always seemed like the hallways down below the main hospital were in need of repairs. It gave the entire place a creepy feeling to it.

Footsteps echoed against the floor, making a rhythm to accompany the mournful squeaking of the one bad wheel.

The doors were metal and were on hinges. There was so little security in the basement. There was no need for it. Security cameras were all the precautions they took down there, and a guard at the top of the elevator to take names. The stairs were for emergencies only and even they had more security features around them than the actual office.

The gurney pressed against the swinging doors easily, pushing them open to allow the intern and the patient on the gurney to enter the room.

The plaque on the wall read "morgue".

The room was brightly lit, far brighter than the hallway outside. The walls were painted white and the fixtures were all shiny brushed steel. The lights were pot lights, with long pendant style lights hanging over the fixed metal autopsy tables. The back wall was made up of brushed steel doors, row upon row, in columns. They were all closed firmly and none had tags to indicate that they were full.

There were already two morticians awaiting the arrival of the intern and the gurney. Both men were dressed in their drab green scrubs with pristine white lab coats over top. They already had their gloves on and the surgical instruments that they intended to use were spread out on several rolling tables. Vials and Petrie dishes and needles were there as well. The morticians were instructed to take as many samples as they could get.

The intern shifted nervously.

"Are you staying?" the first mortician asked gruffly. He had dark hair and blue eyes. He was clean-shaven, though his hair was longer, a modern cut for a middle aged man. He was about five-foot-eleven, trim and fit. He looked like he could have once been in the military, though the stories he told were insane and totally fabricated, despite what he told you.

"I was told not to," the intern said.

"Then scram," the mortician said grumpily, with a dismissive wave of his hand. "We have no need for you."

The intern blinked but did as he was asked and scurried away. The doors swung against one another with a noise that sounded like heavy cardboard swishing against itself. The two morticians stood there in silence as they waited for the doors to stop moving. When the doors stopped, and the morgue was wrapped back in the eerie silence it so welcomed, the morticians began to move.

The one who hadn't spoken unzipped the body bag, revealing their subject. A look of pain and sorrow crossed his face as he looked upon the cadaver, still wrapped in the hospital gown and the black vinyl of the body bag.

"She was so young," he said quietly, a light British accent touching his words. He was a little taller than the gruff mortician, standing at six-foot-one. His hair was cut short, almost buzzed and he had a five o'clock shadow that seemed to be permanent. His eyes were also blue, but were much paler, with flecks of green and brown in them. He was lanky and rail thin. His eyes were red-rimmed, as though he had allergies, or never slept. Both were applicable. You don't work for years in a morgue and still maintain normal sleep patterns.

He reached for the chart attached to the bottom of the gurney. "Good Lord," he breathed as he read the different reports. The chart was almost as thick as a paperback novel. "She's been through hell."

"Well then, let's hurry this up so that she can get on to her final resting place," the first mortician replied, dispassionately. It wasn't that he didn't care, but he was used to seeing death on a daily basis. The state of their cadaver was a welcome change of pace, however. At least she wasn't horrifying like some of the car wreck victims. Or the shooting victims. Or some of the scarier accidents that happened on construction sites. He wrinkled his nose at the thought.

The British mortician nodded and set the chart on top of the cadaver. He wrapped his arms around her legs, the gruff mortician took her shoulders. They didn't even need to count, they were so in tune and used to one another that they just lifted her. She weighed next to nothing, it seemed, and they lifted her easily and set her gently on the autopsy table. The gruff mortician removed the body bag delicately and folded it up for the next time.

The British mortician frowned as he looked over the chart. "She's had every kind of test run on her," he said sadly, "and they still couldn't fix her."

"This is the one they called 'Zero' isn't it?" the gruff mortician asked. "She was in quarantine for like six weeks. She's been upstairs dying and they didn't know why."

The Brit's eyes grew wide. "This is Zero? Holy shit. Shouldn't we be in hazmat suits or something then?" he asked incredulously.

The first man arched his eyebrow. "You're scared of a corpse?" he teased.

"I'm scared of the virus that did this to her," the Brit replied quietly. "Six weeks with every heavy duty anti-viral medication known to man, every antibiotic, and damn near every test we have run on her with no cure and no idea as to what actually caused it? Don't tell me you're not worried about that."

The other man shrugged. "She's dead now," he said flatly. "The virus is dead too. We'll be fine. Now quit yer bellyachin' and call up Trudy with the camera. We need to record this, get all our samples, you know the drill. They're going to test her until they figure it out." He shrugged and carefully removed the hospital gown from the cadaver and covered the corpse instead with a white sheet.

The Brit wrinkled his nose in distaste but did as he was asked, setting the chart down on the long counter they used as a worktable. He frowned at the microscopes and tools on the flat counter, hating the idea that they were the ones who had to get all the samples. Shouldn't that have been done by the doctors in the quarantine? They could have taken the samples themselves and sent them off for tests and biopsies.

Slowly, he reached for the phone handset that acted as their intercom. He pressed a call button and held the receiver to his ear.

"Hey, Trudy. You and Sean can come in here now. We're about to start and we need the video and an extra pair of hands would be helpful," he said quietly. "Thank you," he added before hanging up the phone. He sighed and eyed the biohazard signs on all of the equipment that they were supposed to use in collecting their samples.

Something didn't sit quite right with him.

"Look, Mike, this really doesn't seem right to me," the Brit said quickly, wanting to get his thoughts out before the younger morticians arrived with the video. "Something about this seems wrong."

Mike turned his eyes up to his partner. "What are you saying, John?" he asked, his gruff voice betraying his impatience. "That you want to walk out on what could be the most important medical discovery of our lives? You don't wanna be a part of the autopsy that could blow the lid off of this virus? Think about it, man! We have the first victim of a deadly plague here. We're going to have Nobel prizes by next year."

John hesitated. The thought of becoming famous, of getting recognition as a mortician was too tempting. Slowly, he nodded.

"All right then," Mike said. "Now get your head in the game, this is going to be a long and painful one."

John sighed as the doors swished open. The noise was grating on his nerves. He still wasn't entirely convinced that they would be famous, and he still wasn't positive that they all wouldn't be thrown in quarantine for six weeks after this autopsy.

Viruses don't just disappear when you die.

Trudy and Sean entered with quietly mumbled greetings and immediately set themselves up. Sean was shorter than the doctors, with pale hair to match his pale skin. He looked like a thin computer geek and wore it proudly. He had thin, wire-rimmed square glasses that didn't entirely suit his roundish face, and he was dressed in the same drab scrubs.

Trudy was tall, slender and very curvaceous, with vivid, naturally red hair. She was Doctor Summers' personal assistant, hand-picked from the nursing staff and John didn't trust anything that Mike said about the woman. She was dressed in the darker nurse's scrubs, but she only worked in the morgue with Doctor Summers.

Sean was manning the camera that would record the entire autopsy, and Trudy was the assistant to John and Mike. The four of them crowded around the autopsy table as Mike picked up the scalpel.

"We're rolling, Doctor," Sean said with a thumbs up.

"I am Doctor Michael Summers. We are here with 'Patient Zero', the unfortunate girl who has been ill and in quarantine for the past six weeks. Her case number is zero-five-five-six-one-nine and we have been instructed to call her 'Jane Doe' if we do not wish to use the title of 'Patient Zero.' Assisting me today, I have Doctor John Friesen, Nurse Trudy Moseley and on camera is Sean Weathers, our intern and PR specialist."

No one spoke, but simply acknowledged the camera.

Mike continued, "I am going to begin by having Doctor Friesen swab the deceased's mouth, nose, eyes and fingers for bacterial residue. The more we can learn from this case the better."

Doctor Friesen did as he was instructed, handing the capped vials with the swabs inside to Trudy, who immediately put them in biohazard bags and labeled them. She set them aside in a tidy pile. The labs would likely be busy with these samples for weeks. Patient Zero's case had been all over the news; her decline was a public interest story and a warning to anyone travelling abroad. And of course, the conspiracy fanatics had gone nuts over it.

"I am now going to begin with a 'y' incision," Doctor Summers said calmly into the camera.

The others backed off slightly, giving Mike the elbow room he needed to perform the incision. There would be plenty of time for everyone to get their hands dirty. Organs needed to be harvested, biopsies taken, everything needed samples and documentation.

Mike drew back the white sheet he'd so carefully placed against the corpse, revealing the mottled, ruined flesh of the unfortunate Patient Zero. Even the cadaver looked like it was suffering. Everyone knew what sort of trauma the poor woman known as Patient Zero had gone through in life.

The room held its collective breath as the silver of the scalpel's blade flashed in the air. Mike leaned forward, carefully pressing the blade against the thin flesh of the dead woman on the table. Mike's eyes betrayed no emotion as he pressed the blade harder into the dead flesh. There was no emotion there, only concentration.

The scalpel penetrated flesh easily, like a warm knife through butter. He barely cut two inches into the incision before he stopped.

"Mother of God," Mike breathed.

Thick, blackish blood seeped freely from the wound.

"Dead people don't bleed!" Mike exclaimed.

Worry flashed behind the Doctors' eyes and they exchanged a momentarily panicked look.

"She's alive?" Trudy asked, confused.

"Cover her!" John exclaimed. "Quickly!"

Mike reached for the sheet he'd removed only moments before, draping it back over what he had thought was a cadaver.

"I'm sorry!" he exclaimed. "Patient Zero, I'm sorry, we thought... We thought you were dead!" He was stammering, rambling in fright. "If you can hear me, I am so so sorry."

"Trudy," John said steadily, "call upstairs, tell them there's been a mistake. Sean, keep the camera rolling, this is important." He spoke levelly as he gave instructions. He grabbed a gauze pad from the table of supplies and tore it open. "Mike, step back," he said firmly.

Shaking, Mike did as he was instructed.

John stepped forward and placed the gauze against the bleeding incision below Jane Doe's collarbone. "Can you hear me?" he asked.

A low groan escaped from Jane Doe's mouth. It was an inhuman sound, guttural and low. Trudy whimpered at the sound of it and Mike shuddered.

"God, John, she was dead," Mike stammered, placing his hand against his mouth.

John nodded. "We all thought so," he said quietly, staring at the patient on the slab. He reached over and lifted her eyelid. Her eye was milky, clouded over and yellowish, but it moved.

"She's aware!" John exclaimed. "At least, responsive, anyway."

Another low groan escaped Jane Doe's mouth and her arm shot up, grabbing John in her skeletal hand.

"Oh God!" John shouted, startled.

Fingers grabbed, digging into his flesh, far stronger than they should be for someone who had been dead not moments before. Patient Zero pulled herself up, groaning inhumanly. Her eyes snapped open, and she turned her head to stare at the Doctor she was holding. A hissing, rattling inhalation came from her as she pulled herself up.

"We're sorry!" John exclaimed. "Calm down, you've been through..."

His sentence was cut off as a scream escaped his throat. Teeth dug in through the lab coat and warm blood spurted across the white sheet covering Patient Zero.

Trudy screamed.

John's face went as white as his lab coat and Patient Zero's hand grasped his throat. Another inhuman groan and she pulled him down, her teeth finding his neck. His scream was cut short, turning into a gurgle as dark blood poured from his mouth. His eyes rolled back in his head as his last breath escaped him.

"Oh my God! Oh my God!" Sean shouted, grabbing his camera and backing up.

Trudy was still screaming.

Thinking quickly, Mike grabbed a metal tray, sending the tools sitting on it clattering to the ground as he hit Patient Zero over the back of the head. The clanging reverberated off the walls as he struck her again and again.

"What the fuck?" Sean asked loudly, his voice high pitched.

"Trudy, call for help," Mike demanded.

Trudy stopped screaming long enough to nod and make the call.

"What the hell was that?" Sean demanded, still holding the camera.

"I haven't the faintest idea," Mike said weakly. He let the tray drop from his hands and he walked around the autopsy table. He grabbed John by the shoulders and rolled him over, intending to get a better look at the wound on his throat.

John groaned as Mike rolled him over. Mike wasn't quick enough to react and John was on his feet, teeth gnashing as they sunk into the flesh of Mike's face. Mike's scream was louder than Trudy's, blood curdling and pained as the undead John propelled them both back against the counter where Trudy was standing.

Trudy stumbled as she tried to get away from the biting, bloody, screaming tangle of the doctors, only to find herself face to face with the reanimated Patient Zero.

She didn't even have time to scream.

Sean slipped on the floor, landing in the blood pooling around him. The camera he had held on to clattered to the ground, still filming as the naked, reanimated corpse of Patient Zero approached him.

"Oh God..." Sean begged, crying as dead fingers grabbed at him.

His screams echoed the loudest down the hall. Help was just arriving. The men who worked hospital security, and another doctor rushed into the room in time to see Trudy and Mike stand up from their bloody places on the floor, throats and faces and torsos torn open, bleeding, entrails spilling from torn bellies. No one should be able to be walking after wounds like that.

The men were too in shock to scream as the corpses moved towards them. They didn't even make a sound as their flesh was torn apart...

Kiriyama

Acknowledgements

It's shocking to me, to have this book put out after all the emotional turmoil it put me through to write the damn thing. I'd definitely like to thank my family for putting up with my moodiness while I wrote this, I know I'm awful, so thanks for coping with me. I would also like to give a huge thank you to my friends, Red, Painter, Ellie and James for pushing me just that little extra bit to get me to finish this one and get me out of my comfort zone.

Finally, thank you, whoever you are, for picking up a copy of this book. It means the world and I hope you enjoy it.

All my love.

-Kai Kiriyama

About the Author

Kai Kiriyama is a writer of many things, mostly novels, of varying genres.

With diplomas in tea leaf reading, palmistry, crystal divination, and crystal healing, it's no surprise to see novels reflecting the otherworldly with her name on them. Influenced by tales of magic, deception and monsters, Kai takes her genre-hopping seriously.

She currently lives in Canada with her pet snake and a looming deadline.

She can be reached by email at kai@theraggedyauthor.com

Find her website at www.theraggedyauthor.com
On Facebook at facebook.com/authorKaiKiriyama
On Twitter twitter.com/RaggedyAuthor

Other Books by Kai Kiriyama

Blaze Tuesday and the Case of the Knight Surgeon

Blaze Tuesday is New York's best PI, but when he takes the case of the murder of a doctor doing charity work for underprivileged kids, Blaze uncovers more than just a world of fashionable robotic body parts.

My Life Beyond the Grave: The Untold Story of Vlad Dracula

Having lived for hundreds of years, it only seemed right that Vlad Dracula would want to share his story. A memoir, written like a conversation with an old friend, giving a glimpse of the life the infamous Dracula once lived, one bite will have you thirsting for more.

Both books are available through smashwords.com and in print through CreateSpace.com

40839841R00066

Made in the USA
Charleston, SC
18 April 2015